AND THEN THERE WERE BONES...

ADRIANA LICIO

The Home Travellers
Press

AND THEN THERE WERE BONES

Book 0 in *An Italian Village Mystery* Series
By Adriana Licio

Edition I
Copyright 2019 © Adriana Licio

Cover by Wicked Smart Designs
Editing by Alison Jack

To Fellow Mystery Readers,
All Over the World.

CONTENTS

PROLOGUE

Dearest Giò,

You will have a good laugh when you receive this. In fact, I'd love to see your face as you read it. I'm afraid your quest for freedom has infected me too: I'm closing my beloved café and quitting Turin. I've bought a nice guesthouse in a gorgeous place: on the splendid Island of Pino, in my native Calabria. So I'll be not far from your family in Maratea.

Turin has given me much, but I need a change of rhythm, a closer contact with nature, and mostly peace. Not in mortal doses, though, which is why I'm not becoming a recluse. Rather, I plan to invite guests for retreats, both short and long, on the island.

For the grand opening, I'm organising a visit for the press on the weekend of 8–10 June. There will be journalists and travel writers from all over Italy, but in addition I would like to take your sister's suggestion on board and invite you and Dorian, since I hope to reach the English market too.

It will be a rather unusual stay for two reasons. As challenging as it may sound, I will ask all my guests to participate in a digital detox programme, and the use of mobiles and internet will be limited to the after dinner hours (if they're really needed at all). Also, Alessandra Romano will be with us – the theatre actress and author – and for this particular weekend, we are organising a game along the lines of Agatha Christie's *And Then There Were None*. Alessandra has written a brilliant murder mystery for our guests to solve, which will help with both the marketing of my new activity, making the launch easier – murders are so popular, aren't they? – and filling the void that some guests might be dreading when TV and internet are cut from their lives.

I enclose the programme and the instructions on how to reach us. Let me know the time of your arrival so that I can arrange for a boat to bring you to the island. I do really hope you can be amongst our guests.

SINCERELY YOURS

BIANCA BELARDI

PART I

FRIDAY

1

PASSENGERS TO THE ISLAND

"*H*i, *this is Filippa. I'll be away without access to my mail or my mobile until Tuesday 12 June. Leave a message and I will get back to you on my return.*"

With that message recorded to her voicemail, she was officially away for the weekend.

Filippa Fumagalli tucked a bang of her pale blonde hair behind her ear. Not wishing to be inundated by calls on her return the following Monday, she had decided it was better to indicate her return would be Tuesday instead. She looked out of the train window, her grey eyes reflecting glimpses of the great expanse of the sea, wishing she could look at this weekend as the beginning of the summer and the so-longed-for holiday time. The magazine had had a rough time recently, with the economic crisis striking hard and the owners asking for results that even the most committed journalists could no longer deliver. They had nonetheless strived to do their best, including working most Saturdays and even Sundays, and since September of the previous year, she had basically had no break whatsoever. She would even have been looking forward to this weekend away, but for the fact that Ivo Valli Della Volpe would be there. The mere idea of seeing her estranged husband was raising old tensions in her.

Years had passed since their separation, which had never been formalised into a proper divorce – not because they ever imagined rekindling their relationship, but rather as a warning to think twice were either to believe they wanted to marry someone else. Or maybe it was simple carelessness on both sides. Whatever.

Filippa knew people who, after their separation, not only managed to maintain a good relationship, but also claimed that a real friendship had come about as a result, their divorced life ending up being their best time together. This was not the case for her and Ivo.

A POWERFUL MOTORBIKE HIT THE ROAD WITH ALACRITY, BEND AFTER bend, the windy route almost deserted, the tourist season yet to come. If the weather remained fine, a number of day-trippers would come to spend a day on the beach on Sunday, but this Friday it was quiet, and Bruno Scuccimarra could sustain a speed well beyond the allowed limits. He knew there were few risks of speed control on the State Road Tirrena 18 and he found the prospect of spending the weekend in this part of the country alluring: a privilege not to be missed.

To tell the truth, Bruno had been concentrating so hard on the asphalt and the correct trajectories for taking each bend at maximum speed, he had completely forgotten to appreciate the beauty of the landscape. To make up for his negligence, he stopped in a small parking area along the road, removed his helmet, and finally let the wild beauty of this corner of the Mediterranean sink in. He was on the Maratea coast, a 20-minute drive away from Praia a Mare, with rough mountains plunging vertically into the sea from a height of a few hundred metres.

Even the road itself was a sight to behold, curved into the rocky walls almost 100 metres above the blue waters.

He looked at himself in the motorbike mirror and passed his hands through his flattened brown hair to pull it back into shape – a pointless task as the helmet would flatten it again soon. He then took a look at his figure, the black motorcycle leathers hiding his belly and giving him a certain gritty look he wished he could retain when wearing ordinary clothes. Perhaps he shouldn't ask for perfection.

He mounted his motorbike, felt the usual thrill when he switched on the powerful engine, and started his ride, this time at a much more relaxed speed, his eyes finally on the coastline. A few kilometres later, when the greenery of shrubs and holly oaks opened up, he could distinguish, as if carelessly thrown into the blue sea, the grey-green oblong of the Isola di Pino.

GIOVANNA BRANDO WAS HAPPY TO FIND TWO SEATS ON THE BUS ALL to herself, so she could stretch out her long legs comfortably. She appreciated the fact that she could reach the most remote villages in any country in the world by bus and chat with the locals (she found trains much more formal in this respect), but the cramped space often became unbearable after the first three or four hours.

Luckily, this time her bus trip was short. Arriving from London, she had stopped in her hometown, Maratea, for a day to visit her family, and was now on the way to Praia a Mare, a mere 30 minutes along the Tirrenean Coast. Ah, she loved the landscape here, the nice sunny climate. Stupid Dorian should have been with her. But as a Londoner and a dedicated city slicker, he despised rural life in general, and seemed to hate Maratea in particular.

Giò suspected this strong repulsion had something to do with her family. Dorian had never made any secret of the fact he didn't like her provincial relatives. On their side, her family maybe reflected his feelings, but out of respect for Giò, they had never openly shown their dislike. Well, all except Granny. She had been a good match for his pretensions.

A rueful smile brightened up Giò's face. *Not good,* she reprimanded herself. *After all, I'm due to marry him in the autumn. Gosh, at the age of 38!* She smiled even more ruefully. *That's another thing I'm going to have to deal with.*

On this sunny day in June, her thoughts scattered everywhere, leaving her musings over her future life as the wife of a stuck-in-his-ways husband to wonder what was to come in the next couple of days. Not many would have guessed how shy Giò could become on formal social occasions.

If only Dorian was with me. No, he doesn't suffer from shyness at all.

In her mind, she lined up all the people she was going to meet. Ivo Valli Della Volpe, the controversial journalist. At times more a star than a journalist, he was on the covers of so many magazines, more because of his wealth than any professional skills. Bruno Scuccimarra, the man who had travelled most of the globe and written remarkable reports. For sure, he was not as famous as Della Volpe, but still, compared to Giò…

And was Della Volpe's new fiancée, Marinella Martinelli, coming along? More than likely, as she was one of the most famous Italian bloggers around, specialising in fashion and travel with thousands of dedicated fans demanding to follow her minute by minute on Instagram and dreaming of a life like hers.

Giò looked at her jeans and t-shirt. Marinella would doubtless be sporting the romantic look that made such an impression on the Internet. There was not a tiny bit of envy on Giò's side, just the usual feeling of inadequacy.

Damn you, Dorian! Never beside me when I need you.

But Bianca had insisted on Giò joining her for this weekend and she couldn't turn her friend down. She had discovered Bianca's café, Le Torte di Bea, in Turin on a winter's day, years back. The cold in Turin was something she'd never experienced, even in London, and the cosy café, warm and elegant at the same time, had been an unexpected surprise. The glass case inside had displayed a series of pastries on fine porcelain cake stands, each one more inviting than the previous. A cupcake-shaped blackboard promised only the freshest local ingredients, while another one shaped like a steamy cup said, *"Our chocolate is made out of real cocoa. No mass-produced capsules here."* Plants were everywhere: between the tables, cascading from bookcases and shelves of marmalade and preserves. Some chairs were decorated with colourful rose and flower motifs, others had stripes of cream and pink, or the white and blue designs of Dutch porcelain. Despite the fact that the tables and chairs were all different to one another, they somehow managed to mingle in harmony.

After a brunch that had revived her spirits as much as her stomach, Giò had talked to Bianca, the brilliant entrepreneur behind the café, who told Giò her passion was for authenticity and beauty, for finding the freshest, most genuine ingredients, as well as taking care over every detail, be it a cake or a piece of furniture. A true friendship had sprung from that day, and Giò's blog and articles had sent quite a few customers to Bianca's little place. With all this in mind, Giò considered Bianca's new adventure on the Isola di Pino to be one worth exploring and discussing. Finally, courage and curiosity overtook fear and shyness, and Giò, her eyes transfixed by the mixture of mountains and Mediterranean, longed to be on the island.

"OH PLEASE, HONEY, SMILE," SAID MARINELLA, HOLDING HER camera on the selfie stick in front of her and the driver's faces while the wind ruffled their hair. They were in a cabriolet, driving fast on the road to Praia a Mare, and she was determined to show her fans how gorgeous it all was: the car, the landscape, and mostly her new Christian Chor sunglasses and the latest 47 Murderous Red lipstick by Carnel. And, of course, her fiancé.

"Any good?" Ivo asked.

"They will love it!" she replied while composing the text that would accompany the photo. *"Another incredible weekend waits for us. We're heading for Murder Island on a secret mission: discover who the villain is and try not to get killed in the process. Due to the island conditions, I might not be able to speak to you very often, but I'll do my best to send you a few sneaky peaks in the evenings. Everything will be revealed on Monday. In the meantime, can you guess where we're heading?"*

Ivo had asked her not to divulge where they were, just in case hordes of curious people turned up and got in the way. She had sulked for a while, then agreed to disclose everything only at the end of their stay.

She had been born to be a star: she loved to have all eyes on her. To be acclaimed, to be admired or to be envied – it didn't matter. The important thing was to be at the centre of attention. And Ivo? Well, Ivo was not that different, after all. He just pretended to be a bit more mature, which was no great surprise. At the top end of his 40s, he was double her age.

2

L'ISOLA DI PINO

At the station, Giò got down from her bus and spotted a
young brunette waving at her.

"You're Giò Brando, aren't you?"

Giò nodded. "And you must be Caterina."

"Yes, I'm here to take you and the other guests to the island.
We need to wait a few more minutes for the train from Naples to
get here, with Ms Fumagalli on it. Mr Scuccimarra has already
arrived, he has gone to park his motorbike in a garage nearby.
He will be here soon."

"How about the other guests?"

"Mr Valli Della Volpe and Ms Martinelli will be waiting for us
at the pier. They are leaving their car in a parking spot nearby
and wanted to take a few pictures of the coastline and the Fiuzzi
Tower."

A man in unmistakable black motorcycle leathers joined them
and shook hands with Giò.

"You write travel guides, don't you?" he asked her after the
introductions.

"As a matter of fact, I do, though I wish I could write travel
books as you do, but it's not easy nowadays to come up with an
innovative idea…"

"Believe me, travel guides are much more useful than travel books," he said, smiling.

Giò was not to be put off.

"Then I wish I could write useless stuff!"

He laughed, and she smiled back.

A train whistled to announce its arrival, and a few minutes later, Filippa joined them. She looked a bit uncertain, then recognising Bruno, she hugged him tenderly.

"I was so happy that Bianca invited you too." Then she turned towards Giò and Caterina, introducing herself. "I'm Filippa Fumagalli, I'm so pleased to meet you." Her smile was sincere, her handshake more robust than her delicate, pale complexion might have suggested.

They reached the pier by taxi. At its furthest end, two figures were standing close to a fishing boat, embracing while a mobile phone mounted on a selfie stick took packs of shots.

"That's ridiculous." Filippa mouthed the words, thinking they would not be noticed, but Giò saw her, as well as spotting the shadow that was cast over her smile.

When the impromptu photo shoot was over, the couple approached the rest of the group and introductions were made all round. Ivo and Filippa kissed each other's cheeks rigidly while those most abused expressions 'Hello, dear', 'You look well', 'Any news?' flew between the two of them. Bruno expressed his admiration for Ivo's work, but the latter ignored the compliment. Marinella and Filippa didn't shake hands, just nodded and exchanged false smiles.

As the group turned to move towards the dock, Marinella said to Ivo, "Gosh, I thought Filippa would be younger," and made sure everyone could hear her.

"Let's move onto the launch," Caterina said, inviting them on board an open white motorboat.

"Are you driving?" Bruno asked.

"I am. I've known this coast since I was a child," Caterina replied.

"Shouldn't there be one more guest?" Bruno again.

"Mr Cantisani could not make it, but Bianca has arranged for another guest to join us instead. He will arrive late this afternoon."

"Wonder who he is."

"I didn't catch his name," Caterina replied, winking at Giò.

So this last minute guest was to be a surprise. *Who could he be?* Giò wondered.

Caterina expertly manoeuvred the boat out of the bay and Giò's eyes moved from the island to the horizon, and from there to a pack of threatening clouds gathering over the sea.

Caterina confirmed her fears. "Unfortunately, bad weather and rough seas are forecast for tomorrow, but by Sunday afternoon, the sea should calm down and you'll be able to go back home at the agreed time."

"In any case, the island is not too far from the coast," Bruno said.

"When the sea's rough, distance does not make a difference. The waters around the island are extraordinarily perilous. In fact, there's only one dock, as no other part of the island is safe for mooring because of shallow rocks."

"I heard there are a few caves to explore," Bruno continued, watching the island growing larger and larger.

"They're OK with rowing boats, or even better with a kayak or canoe, but with a launch like this one, it's better to keep a safe distance. If you're not too tired, we can have a short tour around the island now since it won't be possible to use the launch tomorrow. It will not take more than 10 to15 minutes."

They all nodded in agreement.

GIÒ'S EYES WERE GLUED TO THE MASS OF THE ISLAND. THERE WAS something imposing about it, despite the sunny day. Its northern part was the wildest, characterised by dark grey rock walls plunging into the waters from an impressive height of 80 metres. From below, she could hardly see the summit of the island, which towered 100 metres above them. The ruins of an ancient tower showed it had been a strategic viewpoint for centuries.

The southern part of the island was greener as it was covered by a thick blanket of vegetation: shrubs, holly and carob trees. From the sea, the green mantle looked so complete and unviolated that Giò could hardly imagine their guesthouse lay somewhere in there.

"This is the Cascades Grotto," said Caterina, manoeuvring slightly closer to the rocks.

"Why is it called that?" asked Marinella, shooting a video.

"Today, the sea is too rough to hear them, but there are waters running throughout the vegetation, making a continuous noise like a cascade. Maybe, if you return another time in more favourable weather conditions, we could arrange a kayak ride. We already have a few booked for our summer guests."

The Blue Grotto was the one they managed to get closest to, it being the largest. It was a real show of crystal-clear sapphire waters, which turned indigo and navy as they progressed further inside.

"Can't we go in?" begged Marinella.

"Not with these currents," Caterina said, shaking her head.

A few more metres and they reached a natural harbour inside a small inlet. A little stony wall acting as a pier sheltered it further from the currents so the boat was safely protected in case of rough sea.

Caterina secured the boat with the help of Bruno, then pointed towards an egg-yolk-yellow Ape car.

"You can put all your luggage in there, I will take it to the house which is about 600 metres from here. I can take one passenger with me if you don't fancy walking."

"Filippa, dear, I think you should take the lift," Marinella said.

"Although I may seem like an ancient mummy to a little baby

like you, I can assure you that I enjoy walking. But I appreciate your consideration." And Filippa returned the falsest smile ever.

"Let's go," said Bruno with an appreciative look at Filippa.

"Caterina, can't you take us all the way up if we sit with the luggage?" Marinella asked as Bruno and Filippa strode away.

"I'm afraid the road is too steep for that."

"Then just let us shoot a short video of the first 20 metres. It will give our fans such a feel for the island and the adventure."

"Marinella, love, is this necessary?" Ivo asked, looking at the small space left on the Ape. He was rather a tall man and Giò could hardly imagine him sitting in the back of the vehicle, especially now it was crammed with luggage.

She shrugged. "Of course it is, you silly. Giò, would you take a few shots for us? I'll show you how to do it. Please, Ivo, sit in there. Caterina, we need to take a few shots with the stopped vehicle, I'll tell you when you can start moving. Such a pity Bruno has walked away, I suspect he's a better photographer than you are, Giò."

Giò had too much of a sense of humour to be touchy and she enjoyed the good 20 minutes that followed. Marinella cried, hugged, thanked, directed all her 'staff', checked the resulting photos and videos, and only when she was absolutely satisfied with the results did she let them go. It was a mystery how a person could manage to be that self-absorbed and treat all people as if they had no other purpose in life than to fulfil her desires.

Wish I could be even 10% as in love with myself as Marinella, rather than thinking I might be a nuisance all the time.

Giò, who normally loved walking, accepted the lift in the Ape.

"I suspect Ivo and Marinella will take ages to arrive at the house, each step needing at least five selfies," she joked with Caterina.

"Dearest Giò!" Bianca cried, hugging her. "It's been such a long time."

"I can't believe you did it!" said Giò, returning the hug and looking at her friend with sincere admiration. "I thought you loved that café and would never let it go."

"Life is so full of choices. But you're right, 'Le Torte di Bea' was my own creation, and it was hard to let it go. But I'm 60 and want to enjoy my life before I need someone to look after me."

"Come on, you're as fit as ever. Actually even better than usual." Giò's compliment was sincere: the contact with nature had done Bianca the world of good. Her skin was looking healthy and slightly tanned, and she was one of those women who never neglected herself. Her dark hair was nicely combed, her figure looked slender, and though she was dressed for the outdoor life, she was as stylish as ever. But she never overdid it. Taking care of herself was second nature to her.

"And when you eat by yourself, I bet you still lay the table," Giò teased, acknowledging she was the opposite of her friend, but appreciating their differences.

"I do! In the evenings, I may even light candles, play some soft music, drink a glass of red from my favourite wine glass."

"And cook the perfect meal."

"Simple, but prepared with love," Bianca admitted.

"I've not met many people who love cooking for themselves. We mostly end up with frozen or microwaved food."

"Never!" Bianca shook her head vigorously and squinted her eyes, abhorring the idea.

"So you're going to become a hermit?"

"Oh no. Although I confess I've started to enjoy my solitary spells, I still love to have people around. I've found good staff to help me with the guesthouse. And when the season is over, I will relax, travel a lot and plan for the new season from afar."

When Giò turned, a tall, imposing woman was standing close to the main entrance. Wavy blonde hair cascaded down her back; full lips were highlighted by a deep red lipstick; green eyes, a generous bosom, slender waist, and long, elegant legs were complemented by a slinky red dress.

"This is Alessandra, she's helped me to organise the murder."

Giò laughed at the unusual introduction. "Good to meet you. I might need your help sooner rather than later."

Alessandra rolled her eyes and, smiling, shook Giò's hand. "Bianca is giving me a hard time, referring to me as the Murder Woman at the local market, so don't be surprised if the police arrive on the island, hunting for me."

"If they don't arrest you, do you plan to stay here for the season?"

"I live in Naples, but during the summer season I'd love to organise dramatised events on the island whenever Bianca and her guests want them. And by that, I don't only mean murders."

"A murder is always a more appealing theme for a weekend away than a romance or family saga, though," Bianca said.

Bruno joined them. "Sorry to interrupt..." He paused, mouth open in surprise, unable to tear his eyes away from Alessandra. If women perhaps saw that, in her 50s, she was a fading beauty, the structure of her cheekbones helped by a doctor, her lips artificially filled, he only noticed the tall, voluptuous figure, the long blonde hair and sensuous voice, all of which made Alessandra the archetype of the *femme fatale*. It took him a good minute to recover and be able to introduce himself to both the owner and her 'murder woman'.

"So Filippa has also arrived, has she?" said Bianca cheerfully. "Let's go onto the terrace outside where we've prepared a simple welcome cocktail before we accompany you to your rooms."

"WHO ARE THEY?" GIÒ ASKED BIANCA AS THEY REACHED THE terrace, pointing to two cats who were looking disdainfully down on the guests from a whitewashed wall covered with purple bougainvillea.

"The black one is Thunder, and the tortoiseshell one is Storm. They're feral cats, but I'm determined to win their hearts. As aloof as they can be, they seem quite curious about all these weird people."

"You mean they lived all alone on the island?"

"Yes. Since the previous owners left, there was nobody taking care of them, but there's plenty of prey. Actually, they spurn all the packaged food Caterina has offered them."

"Packaged food? What horror! Of course you get along with them." Giò laughed, scratching a long branch on the terracotta floor of the terrace and attracting Storm's attention. The cat's tail swished as if she was about to pounce. Their eyes met, and Giò said, "We'll become friends."

The guests were all gathered on the terrace. A white table was set in front of them, decorated with broom flower arrangements. Trays were filled with colourful bruschetta overflowing with tomatoes, garlic, basil and oregano; fritters of aubergines, zucchini flowers and anchovies; and small arancini di riso, containing rice mixed with pesto and pecorino. And it was all accompanied by sparkling prosecco.

"I don't want to spoil your appetite before dinner, so I only prepared light food."

"She's a bit on the motherly side, I'm afraid," said Alessandra, smiling at Bianca.

"That's very true. If I go too far, please let me know."

"Indeed, I might have something to say about limiting the use of mobiles while we're on the island," Marinella moaned promptly.

"As for that, I'm afraid I'm immovable. I want people to enjoy speaking to each other, live their stay to the full, and I totally abhor selfies."

"She's so old fashioned," Alessandra said indulgently. "But as you'll experience exactly the same frustrations as the guests who will be coming over after you've gone, you'd better alert them to the risks."

Marinella looked at Alessandra, suspicious of her friendly manner. She considered Filippa and Bianca too old, Giò's figure too sporty to be attractive, but the actress constituted open competition. Marinella was aware that Ivo had responded to Alessandra in the same way as Bruno: they seemed hypnotised by her. No, the actress's pleasingly cordial manner would not convince Marinella that she didn't pose a threat.

A small woman came out from the kitchen, bringing one more tray of arancini straight from the pan. Before she could slip away again, Bianca introduced her to the guests.

"This is Carmela, Caterina's mum. She's our cook – she's got magic hands with any kind of food."

Carmela bowed her head shyly to them all, but beyond her humble demeanour, she shared the same strong features as her daughter. Dark hair and an expressive square face softened by almond-shaped brown eyes shining through dense eyelashes.

"So there are eight of us, plus Caterina," said Bruno, counting the heads. "Are we nine little Indians and not ten?"

"The tenth is coming. Mr Cantisani pulled out at the last minute, but I found a worthy substitute," Bianca explained. All eyes were on her as she laughed mischievously. "And I won't tell you who that person is until he's here. Caterina has gone back to Praia to pick him up."

"Good, so there will be exactly ten of us, and the story has already started," Bruno said, indulging in one last arancino.

"More of that at dinner time," Alessandra said with her finger in the air as if pointing to something going on above her. The men smiled at her, while Marinella looked on sulkily.

"I'm glad the new guest is a man," she told Giò. "There're too many women and too few men, and that's going to be a problem."

"Why?" asked Giò, genuinely intrigued.

Marinella rolled her eyes. There was no way a sporty woman would understand what life was about.

"There's a tigress who's definitely hunting for men," she said as she gestured towards Alessandra, who was walking towards them. Then, as if it was nothing, Marinella added, "And there's Filippa possibly wanting to get her hubby back."

"But as I understand it, they've been divorced for quite a long while," Alessandra said, joining the conversation. "And you're with him, now."

Marinella replied icily, "Most women don't care if a man has moved on and is in a relationship or not, they prey on what they can get, regardless. As for Filippa and Ivo, they never actually divorced, but I mean to make sure he does so as soon as possible. I can keep my eyes wide open when I need to." And she gave Alessandra a meaningful look that the older woman decided to simply ignore.

When the trays were empty and the glasses dry, Bianca invited her guests to get some rest.

"I'd say I've kept you here long enough. I'll accompany Marinella and Ivo to their rooms. Carmela, could you show Filippa and Giò to theirs? Giò's staying in the tower room – she'll enjoy the best view from there. Bruno, come along with me, you're staying in the same wing as us."

"But I'd love a room with a view," Marinella said, looking sullen. She moved her eyes from Giò to Ivo, uncertain where she should be looking as the latter was gazing too much and too often in Alessandra's direction.

Bianca replied dryly, "Giò's got a small single room, so unless you want to split from your sweet other half…"

Marinella instantly backed off. "Of course not, I didn't know that."

"I'm sure Giò can cope with a smaller room if it's got a worthwhile view. Filippa, in your case I thought you'd favour comfort, so yours is a large, airy room."

Filippa nodded. "Whatever you've chosen, I'm sure it will be perfect. I'm not one to whine."

Bianca, used to dealing with children's tantrums, said, "And you, Marinella, will find your room very romantic with a nice view towards the coast." Then she added, "Dinner at 8.30. After dinner, Alessandra will explain the rules of the murder mystery. I can only hope you're not too… sensitive!"

WHEN GIÒ REACHED HER ROOM, TO HER SURPRISE, SHE DISCOVERED there was a double bed and the room was large and airy. And being a sort of tower at the end of a corridor, it had windows on three sides.

She laughed and turned to Carmela. "I won't let Marinella know about this."

"Mrs Bianca is always taking risks – I don't know how she does it. I'd get so confused; I prefer to tell the truth at all times. Not because I'm necessarily more honest than she is, but I'd be afraid of being discovered."

"I know what you mean," said Giò, "but Bianca's always taken risks in her life, and she can master a few fibs when they're needed. It's never because she's afraid of telling the truth, and that makes her different from a common liar. So Filippa is next to me, but whose room is next to hers?"

"That's Alessandra's. I guess she's busy downstairs preparing some mischief for the dinner. In this wing, there's just the three of you."

"Then I'll keep an eye on our mischievous author."

"She's a lovely and helpful woman. With her looks, I thought she'd have the temperament of a diva, but she's very down to earth." If the last remark was meant as a dig at Marinella, it was subtle.

Before leaving, Carmela asked, "Is there anything else you might need?"

"I'd say everything looks perfect. I'll take a quick shower, then enjoy the view in the last rays of the sun."

3

THE UNEXPECTED GUEST

By eight o'clock, Giò was already in the living room. A light, airy room, the floor made of hand-painted Vietri tiles in bright colours, its three arched doors opened out on to the terrace. Below the dark beams crossing the ceiling were a series of fine white sofas, a dark ebony table, plenty of plants with giant leaves...

All in the best Bianca style, Giò thought.

Bruno and Ivo were chatting next to a tall fireplace made from the local white stone. Actually, Ivo was doing all the talking, boring Bruno about the current state of Italian politics, patronising him. Ivo hadn't interrupted his flow when Giò arrived, but when Alessandra joined them...

"Politicians be damned! What are you going to tell us about the murder mystery?" Ivo asked, not bothering to hide his admiring glance.

"Not much, I'm afraid. Bianca and I will explain everything after dinner."

"Oh, come on, don't be precious. Tell us if we're supposed to recreate Agatha Christie's *And Then There Were None* story or if it will be something new. I've found the *Ten Little Indians* poem in my bedroom – it's rather tenebrous for a nursery rhyme."

"It'd be too easy for you talented sleuths if we used exactly the same story. So answering your question, you'll be playing something totally new, although inspired by Mme Christie's mystery," Alessandra conceded, adjusting the broom and bougainvillea flowers that Bianca had arranged in a white porcelain vase that morning.

Bruno finally managed to get a few words in edgeways. "It was the darkest of Christie's stories. I never realised that until I reread the mystery before coming down here."

Filippa had joined them. "It gives me the creeps," she said. "I mean, we're on an island, just like the characters in that book, and we're going to talk murder. I'm glad we're in sunny Calabria and not gloomy Devon."

Ivo raised the curtains to show her the last crepuscular light dulled by banks of clouds. "Sunny? My dear, you're never in touch with reality. It looks like the storm is catching up with us already. It's gloomy enough here, too, a perfect match for the Devon Island."

"Oh please, I'm not brave, either," Giò said. "So I hope this adventure will have a funny side, or I might end up asking Bianca if I can share her room." Her words managed to break the tension as the others laughed. "But it's true, it is a rather grim tale. Usually, despite the corpses piling up, there's something playful in Christie's mysteries. But no fun in this one at all."

"Let's hope our host will allow us some humour, then." A tall man with almost dead straight hair, piercing grey eyes and a deep, velvety voice stepped into the room. Ivo, as if recognising the voice, turned around too suddenly, hitting Alessandra and knocking the flower vase she was holding in her hands onto the floor.

"That was quite an entrance!" Bruno exclaimed.

"Mr De Giorgis," Giò cried, recognising the famous journalist.

Filippa, taking no notice of the mess behind her, moved towards him.

"Giorgio, such a surprise to see you here."

"Enchanting as usual, Filippa," he said, his admiring glance resting on her slender figure dressed in an elegant blue-grey dress before he hugged her.

"You too. You're living proof that time is a gentleman, but only for men, I'm afraid." Filippa smiled, then turning towards the others, she started the introductions. "This is Bruno Scuccimarra, a travel reporter and good friend of mine."

Talkative Bruno, for once, was speechless with surprise, and only shook hands with the newcomer.

"I'm going to call Caterina to help us to mop up the water," Giò said. "And by the way, Mr De Giorgis, it's such an honour to have you as one of the guests. Bianca said there was a surprise, but we would have never imagined... I'm Giò Brando, by the way."

"That's a fine name! Where are you from?"

"Maratea, sir. Not too far from here, though I've been living in London for the past 10 years." She looked behind him at the mess. Alessandra was bending down to the floor, gathering up the pieces of the shattered vase.

"Don't you worry, Giò," Bruno said, "I'll call for Caterina."

"That was an entry with a fanfare!" Filippa smiled.

Ivo was helping Alessandra and seemed determined not to turn towards the newcomer.

"I'll clean it up, don't you worry," said Caterina, arriving with absorbent paper and a bucket for the shards of pottery. "I'll see if we can save any flowers."

"Was it me?" Ivo asked Alessandra.

"It's OK, really." She stood up and went to shake hands with De Giorgis. His eyebrows rose as she introduced herself. "I'm Alessandra, an author helping Bianca to entertain her guests."

"I see." His grey eyes scrutinised her. Giò would have wilted under such a glance, but Alessandra seemed to challenge it with a mischievous twinkle in her eyes.

Ah, to be a real woman, Giò thought.

"Have we met before?" he asked.

Alessandra shook her head slowly, her hair swaying sensuously with the movement. "I'm afraid not."

"That's a pity. You have such captivating green eyes, but they would have been brown if they'd been the ones I'm looking for."

She looked at him quizzically and he was about to answer her unspoken question when a piercing scream of surprise interrupted them.

"Oh my goodness! Mr De Giorgis," cried Marinella, arriving on the scene. "So *you* are the unexpected guest." She came forward, ignoring the rest of the group, and shook hands with him. "I'm Marinella Martinelli. I'm… I shouldn't really say it, but I'm a rather famous fashion and travel blogger. I've always dreamed of writing a weekly column for a respected newspaper like yours about fashion; I'm sure it would make most of my fans buy your newspaper. I know the press is in the middle of a huge economic crisis, but I'm a firm believer that new communication styles should meet the old news industry and do good things together."

She certainly knows how to sell herself – remorselessly, Giò thought, amazed at the girl's audacity.

"I'm sure thanks to people like you, Martinella, we'd solve many if not all of our problems," he replied wryly.

"My name's Marinella," she corrected him, uncertain for the first time, "Marinella Martinelli."

"Oh, I apologise, sincerely. But I'm sure it would be rather unfair to annoy people with our little lives, whilst we're in such a pleasant company." He winked at Giò.

"Oh… but… but… certainly. I'm going to ask Bianca to make sure she sits me beside you for dinner. Actually, before I do that, shouldn't we take a selfie together?"

"That, I'm afraid, is a pleasure I'm obliged to deny. Selfies are only good for beautiful ladies. I'm too old for them anyway."

"Surely not! You're not too old, and you're such a handsome man…"

This time he interrupted her brusquely. "No thank you! We'll take a picture all together with the rest of the group at the end of our stay."

"I'm sure I will make you change your mind." Undaunted, Marinella continued to flirt. "But let me go and tell Bianca about the seating for dinner. To think that she said nothing at all about you joining us. That woman!"

As Marinella left, Giò felt she had to complete the introductions. "Mr De Giorgis, this is Ivo Valli Della Volpe, a journalist at the *Banana Gazette*. He's also Marinella's fiancé."

Ivo was still looking in the direction Marinella had disappeared with a rather stern expression on his face. It was De Giorgis who spoke.

"Thanks, Giò, but we already know each other fairly well."

Ivo nodded and they shook hands, distinctly coldly, as Bianca appeared.

"Dinner is served, please come over," she said, and a gong let out a deep DONG!

4

MURDER AS A SIDE DISH

At dinner, De Giorgis sat between Bianca and Filippa. Anticipating her protests, he apologised to Marinella.

"I'm sorry, but I've not seen these friends of mine for far too long and it's time we made up for that."

"I see," the blogger said, but it was obvious she didn't appreciate it, nor the fact that Ivo and Alessandra were talking with an ease that piqued her jealousy. Once again, Marinella was reminded that, despite her age, the actress was a fascinating woman.

At least in a man's eyes.

"Sasha, would you pass me the wine?" De Giorgis said in a language nobody understood – nobody but Alessandra, who interrupted her conversation with Ivo.

"Certainly." She instinctively replied in the same language as she passed him the wine bottle.

"So you speak Russian," Bruno said to her. "How come?"

"I am Russian."

"Really?" Bianca was surprised. "I always thought you were Italian, you have no accent whatsoever."

Alessandra smiled. "It must be because I first came to Italy when I was young, and also actors work a lot on pronunciation and phonetics."

"But how did *you* know?" Bianca asked De Giorgis.

"I lived in Moscow for a number of years as a Russian correspondent. As such, I also spent a long time in Tajikistan. I think we probably met there?" he added, glancing towards Alessandra, who shook her head in denial.

"No, I've never been to Tajikistan. I was born in St Petersburg, then moved to Moscow, and from there to Italy."

"I would never have guessed, your Italian is perfect," said Giò in admiration, knowing how difficult it is to master a language that's not your own.

"What brought you to Tajikistan?" Bruno asked De Giorgis.

"Well, it's actually a very interesting little country. It shares some thousand kilometres of border with Afghanistan and the most incredible things happen there."

"I take it you're referring to drug trafficking," Bruno said. "I was there for a few months and saw the great divide between ordinary people who, especially in the countryside, have a poor and tough life, while those involved in narcotic trafficking are extremely rich and love to show it off. In the capital, Dushanbe, majestic palaces, expensive cars and posh shops abound."

"So you've been there too," De Giorgis said appreciatively, repeating Bruno's question to him. "And what took *you* there in the first place?"

"I'm simply a curious traveller, and the roads and territories that connect Europe with the East have always fascinated me. I was interested in how the Tajik government deployed the international funds they received to stop drug trafficking, and we're talking big money here. But speaking to locals, I soon learnt that though single operations seemed to work well, their efforts were mostly unsuccessful on a larger scale."

De Giorgis nodded vigorously in agreement. "That's typical of Western governments, they do not understand the troubles of the countries they want to help. It's not only drugs, it's the corruption. Most funds are used by the powerful opium lords, who have strong connections with the central government, secret service and army, to cut out smaller competitors. Western assistance ends up doing them a favour and making them richer. You need to understand a country before you intervene, otherwise you're liable to do more damage than good."

It was then that a strange metallic voice silenced them all.

"Good evening, ladies and gentlemen, I hope you enjoyed your dinner—" the guests looked at each other, trying to understand where the voice was coming from "—because what follows might not be as pleasant."

"It's just like the Agatha Christie book!" Marinella cried ecstatically.

"You've been invited to this island by Mrs Bianca Belardi, but even she is unaware of the real reason behind this reunion. She's also unaware that I know her secrets. Yes, dear Mrs Belardi here has killed more than one person in her café Le Torte di Bea by putting arsenic in their desserts."

The guests all looked at the cake they were eating. "Oh my goodness!" Filippa laughed, putting down her spoon.

"The Cannistrò mother and daughter, Carmela and Caterina, killed the old lady they were working for, drowning her at sea while accompanying her to the island.

"Mrs Alessandra Romano plotted a fatal incident on stage in order to pass from understudy to main actress, killing the star under a bright spotlight.

"Ivo Valli Della Volpe, after a heated discussion, you pushed your former chief editor off a balcony in Milan and pretended it was suicide. In reality, you wanted to take his place.

"Bruno Scuccimarra, during your trek in the Arctic, in order to survive, you stole the food from your companions and ran away with the dogs and sledges. You then went on to claim they had already died in the storm.

"Giovanna Brando, when you were in Scotland, you scared Mrs Sue Macduff to death by pretending to be a ghost. You knew she had a weak heart, and that she had left you her castle in her will, and at the time, you were in deep financial difficulties.

"Marinella Martinelli, you thought you were not being watched at a carnival party when you stabbed the world famous blogger Mara Lavagni to death. You left before anyone realised that her red dress was tinged with blood.

"Filippa Fumagalli, you poisoned your boss at the magazine so you could take her place.

"And you, Mr Unexpected Guest—" all eyes turned towards De Giorgis "—you always pretend to be *super partes*, but may I remind you that during your stay in China, you sent to his death, thanks to your friendship with the local mafia, a journalist who had discovered your illegal trafficking of antiquities?

"You're all accused of having committed the most awful murders, but somehow you've managed to get away with them. But not on this island. Here all your sins will finally be uncovered and punished."

A SILENCE FELL AMONG ALL PRESENT. THEN FILIPPA SHOOK HER head.

"You know what?" she said. "If I didn't know we were here for a murder weekend, I'd be scared."

"Despite the absurdity of all the accusations?" De Giorgis asked.

"Despite that, yes."

"Then my congratulations, madam."

They all looked at Bianca who nodded, for once a little complacent over her success. Slowly laughter and chatter filled the room again.

"I thought we'd be given roles to play, I never expected you'd use our real names," Giò said.

"Well, I guess the closer the mystery is to the truth, the greater the fun," Bianca replied. "We don't have to record on vinyl nowadays. With digital recordings and a few adaptations, we can use the same storyline with future guests. And of course I'm talking to you like this only because you're our guinea pigs. In the future, as Alessandra has instructed me, I will just plunge into my role."

"But each group of people will have different pasts," Giò objected.

"For the sake of our story, it doesn't matter," Alessandra explained, her bare arm flexing as she rotated the wine in her glass with a sinuous movement. "Though it seems perfectly tailored to a specific audience, in reality, it doesn't make much difference if you're a librarian or a writer, a magazine editor, a manager, or a lawyer. The adaptations are more in the detail than the plot, though of course I'll be happy to change parts of the story when needed."

Caterina came in with a tray of coffee cups.

"You and your mother don't look like greedy murderesses," Bruno said.

"Never trust appearances!" Caterina reminded him.

"No, you're right. From what I've heard, I've got some rather dangerous people around me. I can well imagine you, Marinella, committing a murder, but Giò and Bianca? You frankly astonish me."

Marinella protested, horrified.

"How about me?" asked Filippa, choosing to leave all her doubts behind and dipping her spoon greedily in a tiramisù with wild berries and mascarpone.

"You're a charming woman and, as with all charming women, very capable of murder."

"Ah, Bruno, that's unfair on me and Giò," Bianca remonstrated, half chuckling.

"I'm sorry, a *faux pas* on my part. What I meant to say…"

But he wasn't able to finish the sentence. Alessandra had suddenly grasped his arm as if asking for help. Her body was shivering and convulsing. Her mouth opened as if she could no longer breathe, as if invisible hands were strangling her. With the last of her strength, she pushed back the chair, wanting to escape, but all her energy left her and she fell to the floor with a final convulsion.

There she stayed.

Still.

"Oh my goodness!" Bianca cried, marching towards her friend's prone body. It was at this moment the guests passed from incredulity to panic.

"You mean it's not part of the game?" De Giorgis cried as he reached out towards Alessandra. Bianca shook her head, gulping. Ivo and Marinella stood stock still, immobilised where they were. Giò joined De Giorgis and Bruno, who were checking Alessandra over.

"But she's still breathing!" the latter exclaimed with relief.

De Giorgis touched her pulse. "Her heart is beating normally."

Alessandra opened her large eyes and winked at them all. "But I'm officially dead, the first victim."

A unanimous protest, mixed with a few sighs of relief, sounded around the room.

"How dare you pull our legs in such an underhand way?" Bruno cried, uncertain whether to be angry or not.

"We couldn't let you go to sleep without at least one good murder," Alessandra said.

After De Giorgis had helped her to rise from the floor, Alessandra took her place at the table as if nothing had happened.

"And now the game rules," she said nonchalantly. "Rule number one: I'm dead, so you cannot question me. You can question anyone else, as long as he or she is still 'alive', but hurry up since quite a few will die, I promise you. Rule number two: after breakfast, Wi-Fi will be shut down and you can give all your mobile phones to Bianca. She will lock them in a security box with the modem. She has one key, Caterina the other – you'd better know that, just in case of an emergency. The mobiles will be returned to you before dinner, but we'd be grateful if you didn't use them *during* meals. The Wi-Fi will also be switched on again then."

Marinella sighed. "It will be so hard on me. It's my life and work."

Alessandra was merciless. "You were told it was a digital detox programme, beside the fun of the murder mystery."

Bianca nodded in approval and Alessandra continued.

"Early tomorrow morning, I'll slip your part of the story beneath your bedroom doors: what you're supposed to do, and details of your crimes."

"Crimes?"

"Well, as you heard on the recording, you're supposed to have committed at least one murder – that's why you're on the island. And that's the key to discovering who the killer may be."

"So, we have to find the equivalent of Judge Wargrave?"

"No, that's where the storyline diverges from Agatha Christie's novel. Our killer has a reason to want to kill one or two of those present, but he or she might be forced, because of the turn of events, to kill more people. But that will depend on how good you are at finding him or her. You have two guesses each. And couples will share two guesses, not four."

"That's so unfair," Marinella whined.

"You're also allowed to ask me three questions…"

"You said we couldn't question you since you're dead," Marinella interrupted with a triumphant look, her teaspoon in the air.

"You cannot question my *character*, but you can question me as the arbiter of the game," Alessandra explained patiently. "It will be up to me to decide whether to reply to your questions. But each question counts independently, whether I reply or not. My advice is to speak to the other players, do some sleuthing about their past, let the game run a bit, and use your questions or guesses only when you have some ideas. Of course, those who

ADRIANA LICIO

have been killed are not allowed to share any of the info they've received."

Bianca turned to Alessandra. "Weren't they supposed to receive their part of the story tonight?"

"Having spent some time with the guests, I've got some new ideas, as I suspected I would, and I'd love to amend part of my story tonight. Only small details, but I might do a little rewriting. Then I'll print the parts out for an early morning delivery."

"Bianca, you looked genuinely scared too," Filippa said. "When I saw your frightened face, I feared it wasn't a joke after all. Are you just a good actress, or were you scared for real?"

"That's a good question, Filippa," Bianca replied. "As a matter of fact, Alessandra insisted that we – the staff – wouldn't know the whole storyline. Of course, I suspected it was a joke, but then she was so convincing, I thought something might have really happened."

"That was an awful trick to play on us, Alessandra," Filippa said, half laughing.

"I'm so sorry." Alessandra tilted her head slightly and added softly, "I confess, the atmosphere had been so tense, I couldn't help myself. Maybe I overdid it." With a feline move, she stretched her arms and back in a strangely elegant yawn. "But I'm a bit tired right now, and I still have some work to do. I hope you don't mind if I go?"

"Not at all" and "Goodnight" the women replied promptly.

"You definitely need some rest, you look exhausted," added Marinella.

The men looked less keen to let her go.

5

A RESTLESS NIGHT

Once in her bedroom, Giò phoned Dorian in London. He was usually a nightmare on the phone – a simple "Are you OK?" and he would end the call abruptly – but when he heard that De Giorgis was on the island, he was stunned.

"I wish I had come now. Maybe I can catch a flight early tomorrow morning…"

Giò was furious. "What? I begged and pleaded with you to come with me, which would have been so nice, but you told me how busy you are. And now just because a celeb is here…"

"Come on, Giò, it's a once in a lifetime chance."

"Exactly, and you missed it." Her voice had turned icy. "The game has been set, the roles have been allocated, and because of the rough seas, no boats can travel to and from the island tomorrow."

"Then I could come to pick you up on Sunday, and you could make the introductions…"

"Don't you dare!" Giò put the phone down. Dorian never knew when to stop digging. Was it the fact that he was British that meant there was such a huge difference between the two of them, or was it simply that he was Dorian, and nationality didn't come into it? In all frankness, Giò suspected the latter. Dorian was a brilliant, charming man, but he could be such an opportunist at times. He behaved that way so naturally that she was convinced he must be totally unaware of the unfairness of it all, but to Giò's straightforward and candid nature, it was hard to come to terms with.

Certainly, her future mother-in-law's adoration of her only son had greatly contributed to his narcissistic character. Gosh, her future mother-in-law! She wasn't going to sleep a wink if she got started on that train of thought.

She looked down from her balcony. The lights were lit in the garden – maybe someone was still outside, so surely it would be fine if she went out for a walk. She needed some air.

Giò had reached the stairs at the front of the right wing of the building, uncertain whether to switch on the lights or use her mobile as a torch, when one of the doors opened. She recognised De Giorgis's silhouette. He didn't switch on the lights either and walked past her, unaware of her presence, going in the direction Giò had come from, only to stop and knock at the second door along the corridor.

Giò's curiosity was aroused and she stopped where she was able to see what would happen next. The door stayed closed, and in the feeble moonlight coming in through the corridor windows, she saw the man making his way back to his room. Giò stood still in the shadows a couple of stairs down while he passed by, once more unaware of her presence.

Was De Giorgis courting Filippa? Not unlikely, but surely the woman knew how to deal with it. It couldn't be new to her.

As De Giorgis shut his bedroom door, Giò resumed her walk downstairs. Once outside, she kept to the edge of the lighted forecourt. She knew someone was outside, but had no wish whatsoever to talk.

She had turned onto a pathway, breathing in the smell of the broom in blossom, when she heard angry voices coming towards her. Maybe it was a sign of her getting old, or maybe she was just a typical village gossip, but before she knew it, she had hidden behind an ancient olive tree.

"How could you be so coquettish with the man who ruined my life?"

"I wasn't being coquettish at all!" a girlish voice shrilled.

"Shh, not so loud!" The man was hissing, sounding like he was finding it a massive effort not to explode. "Wasn't it you who offered to sit next to him? And did he respond? Of course he didn't. In fact, he sat as far from you as possible."

"That I will never forgive him for!" Marinella's sulky voice was impossible to mistake.

"But it's not only that. You do understand he ruined my career? A word from him and I might be sitting as the chief editor of a real newspaper. But no. He's an awful, unscrupulous man; keep away from him. If you can't, then I will have to take matters into my own hands."

The last few words sounded much more threatening than they should have done.

The couple walked towards the house, out of earshot, and Giò was finally left to appreciate the scents of the night on the island. The fresh air soothing them, her thoughts left Dorian and his mother to move on to her companions on the island.

To her surprise, she saw two matching dark-green lights, shining out from under an olive tree.

"Is that you, Storm?" she whispered.

The cat meowed in confirmation.

"We do have a weird party of people, don't we?"

The green lights went out for three seconds, approving her words.

With the help of her phone light, Giò, followed at a distance by Storm, managed to reach the dock. The boat was being swayed by the waters, while the sound of the waves crashing against the outer part of the pier announced that the sea conditions were changing, just as Caterina had warned. From the dock, Giò could distinguish the lights of the coastline and she felt pleasantly separated from the noise and hustle of the mainland, there in the middle of the sea.

When she finally decided it was time to hit her bed, the garden lights were still on. Thinking idly that they were probably photovoltaic so as not to waste energy from the guesthouse's electricity generator, she returned inside and made her way up the stairs.

But the night was doomed to be one of encounters. She was at the top of the stairs, just about to make her way down the left wing corridor, when a door opened. It had to be Alessandra's door, but Filippa came out, the two of them laughing and saying, "Shh".

Once more Giò decided, for no apparent reason, not to make her presence known. She heard Filippa saying, "Don't you worry, I'll be perfect, no one will suspect…" then moving towards her room. After that, the two doors were closed in sync.

So that's why Filippa didn't answer De Giorgis's knock, she wasn't in her room. But what were she and Alessandra discussing for so long in the middle of the night? It would seem I'm not the only restless soul on the island.

Giò spent a while ruminating before her head finally sank into the pillow and she fell into a deep, dreamless sleep.

PART II

SATURDAY

6

MORNING FUN

Early the following morning, a letter was slipped under Giò's door containing all her instructions for the game. She learnt that not only was she the villain who had killed Alessandra at dinner, but she had already claimed another victim during the night: Carmela. Caterina's mother had been a risk as she'd noticed Giò coming into the kitchen the evening before to put poison in Alessandra's dessert, the only one different from the others due to Alessandra's allergy to milk derivatives.

The next victim would be De Giorgis. Giò had to kill him next to the Saracen Tower during the morning walk, stabbing him. There was an explanation of her motives for the murder and an invitation to play her part well, asking questions as if she were a potential victim like all the others. It was a rather complicated story of a rich inheritance and vengeance, not immediately easy to digest, so Giò went through it a few times to make sure she wouldn't give herself away.

When she came down for breakfast, the table was laid, but no noises were coming from the kitchen. It didn't take long before the other guests joined her, and they were chatting animatedly when a distraught Caterina appeared on the threshold. Between heartbroken sobs, she told them that her mother had been killed during the night, suffocated in her bed with a pillow pressed against her face. She announced that the sea was too rough for the police to reach them, and that she'd try to cook something for them, putting aside her pain and strain. They'd have to understand it would be nothing more than a simple breakfast.

This time, there was no panic. The guests teased Caterina for her fortitude; she winked back, but continued to play her part, alternating her lament with gulps of hardly restrained laughter. For their part, the sleuths sat down at the table with healthy appetites and appreciated that the simple breakfast was, in fact, a rather lavish one.

"Please don't touch anything," Marinella rebuked as her companions picked up the cornetti and brioches Caterina had left in the centre of the table. "I'd better take a few pictures and update my socials. Such a pity this silly idea of having our phones taken away is going to restrict me so much. I've got my camera, of course, but I'll only be able to update my Instagram posts twice a day."

By tacit agreement, the others all ignored her and fell upon the food on the table.

"Well, maybe it's a matter of a workplace dispute that's got out of hand," Bruno said, biting into a cornetto dripping with orange marmalade. "Or maybe Bianca decided to kill Alessandra because of jealousy, then she had to do her cook in as well, because Carmela had surprised her lacing Alessandra's dessert with poison last night."

"Why didn't Carmela say anything last night, then?" Ivo asked.

"Because it was common and natural to see Bianca attending to the desserts. It was only overnight that she realised what she had witnessed was Bianca poisoning the dessert, but by then it was too late as Bianca had realised this too. Also, Bianca was the only one beside Carmela herself or Caterina who could have killed Alessandra."

Bianca chuckled.

"But she could have killed Alessandra quietly at some other moment, so why wait for the whole party to be here?" Filippa asked, gesturing for Bruno to pass her the butter.

"It could also have been one of us guests, someone who knew Alessandra already," Giò said, remembering she had to join in the discussion so as not to arouse suspicions. "Either way, I'm sure Carmela was killed because she saw something or someone."

De Giorgis added, as if thinking aloud, "From my balcony, I believe I saw Ivo and Marinella in the garden last night. Maybe they were discussing today's murders."

Ivo almost choked on his ham and cheese toastie. "It's still the same old story: you blaming me for things I haven't done, or faults I don't have."

"Well, you never managed to prove the contrary," was the glacial reply.

Ivo's eyes looked like they would fly out of their sockets at any moment.

"That was a private discussion," Marinella groused at De Giorgis, who continued cheekily, unconcerned by their reaction.

"Your own room would have been a much more comfortable place to do that. I suspect you two were plotting something else."

"How dare you!" Marinella looked furious and Ivo's teeth were grinding. Giò believed for a moment she could actually hear them as well as see the tensing jawline.

"You see, he's never learned to accept criticism of any kind," Filippa muttered caustically.

"I think you're all playing your parts beautifully, thank you," Bianca intervened to restore the peace before things got out of hand. "For today, we had planned a day on the beach, but since the weather is so poor we suggest you have a walk on the island. It's coldish, but no heavy rain is forecast for the first part of the morning. Or you could join me for a yoga class. We'll have a break at 11am when you're free to go back to your rooms and relax. I'm sure despite her loss, Caterina will be able to lay the table for coffee and a light snack. Then at 11.30, we'll join our... ehm... dead cook for a lesson on how to make cavatelli pasta for our lunch."

"Recipes from hell," Bruno said.

"Come on!" Filippa laughed slightly, slapping him on the arm as if he was a naughty boy. Bianca smiled at them both, then continued.

"If you're not a keen cook, there's our library, and a snooker room too."

Alessandra came in with a wicker basket. "The sad moment has come, I'm afraid, to put your mobile phones in here, please. I will also switch off the modem, so from this moment, you're disconnected from the Internet. Watch your backs, the killer might be anywhere. I'd advise you whatever you do to stick to groups of three or more people, but if, despite my warnings, you choose to be alone, be very, very careful."

"Oh please! That sounds so scary, Alessandra," Filippa said. "Yoga, walks, books – even without the murder mystery, I'd still be happy and grateful."

THE MORNING'S ACTIVITIES WERE FINALLY SETTLED. DE GIORGIS, Bruno and Giò went out for a walk to explore the island. Ivo Valli Della Volpe said he would spend his time in the library. Filippa, Alessandra and Marinella joined Bianca for her yoga lesson.

"Hey, love, before you go into the library, come along and take a few pictures of me doing yoga," Marinella said to Ivo.

"I'll fetch the camera," he replied, for once without much enthusiasm.

A cloud appeared on Bianca's face. She had thought about mobiles and the Wi-Fi, but not about cameras. When the couple entered the yoga room, Bianca announced that they could not take pictures during the class.

"You can take a few now, before we get started."

Marinella muttered something about how difficult it was for *common* people to understand the nature of her work. In her white leggings and top, she posed for a few shots, asking the others to be in the background, but when Alessandra appeared in her black training tights and slim-fitted red tank, her loose blonde hair falling onto her generous bust, Marinella suddenly said she had enough pictures.

"Ivo, you can go, love. Relax a little yourself."

Filippa and Bianca winked at each other.

"SHALL WE GO TO THE LIGHTHOUSE FIRST?" DE GIORGIS ASKED HIS companions, Bruno and Giò, who nodded. The day was grey and windy but at least, as Bianca had said, there was no rain.

"A pity there's no sun either," moaned Giò.

"Well, I find this weather gives the whole island a wilder appearance," De Giorgis replied, looking around with a satisfied grin. "It doesn't look too domesticated."

"That's all very well for you," Giò said. "You live in Rome and get plenty of good weather all year round. But I was looking forward to a little southern sun."

"And to showing off a tan back in London!" Bruno teased her.

"Why not?"

"Marinella is lucky – she only has to Photoshop her pictures to look as tanned as she wishes," Bruno said wickedly and they all chuckled.

It took a few minutes to reach the lighthouse: a white building with a black top, sitting on the outer tip of the island. It was small and insignificant, but that only endeared it all the more to Giò who was always more appreciative of the little things than the pretentious, monumental ones. For decades, the lighthouse had done its job well, alerting sailors to the fact that a series of dangerous rocks lay all around, just below the water level. It had been built with the robust local stone and then whitewashed. The lantern had a black iron frame and was surrounded by a platform and balustrade, also in black. To Giò's disappointment, the person-sized door was closed.

Today, there were no boats to be seen on the horizon; the sea was already too rough. The powerful waves crashing against the rocks had a hypnotising effect on them. In silence, they watched the ever-changing pattern of the thundering waves and the foam floating on the waters, their nostrils taking in the salty notes as the thin mist of sea droplets was carried inland by a fierce wind.

"Shall we have a look at the Saracen Tower too?" Bruno asked quietly after a while. The other two nodded with enthusiasm.

"Do we need to pass by the villa?" De Giorgis asked.

"No, there's a path," Giò replied. "Caterina told me they keep it clear of vegetation."

As they moved inland, Giò spotted a wooden sign on their left. The path went from west to east, where the island faced the Calabrian coastline. It rose rapidly from sea level to a height of 80 metres, the first part hidden among myrtle and Mediterranean maquis, the higher part cut into sharp grey rocks falling directly down into the sea. The last few metres proved unexpectedly hard, the wind pushing them in all directions, cutting off their voices whenever they tried to speak. Bruno offered Giò his hand when a gust of wind stronger than the rest threatened to push them off the path. It was not only water waiting down below, but also the rocks they had seen when Caterina had taken them around the island.

"Thank you," Giò said when they were safely within a belvedere facing the tower ruins where they could finally breathe without the wind choking them.

"I didn't imagine the climb would be that bad," De Giorgis said as they moved towards the ruins.

"I hope we don't have to go back the same way," Bruno added.

"No, there's a shorter path going down to the pier. And it's inland so we won't have to worry about tumbling down into the sea," Giò informed them as they entered the tower and looked at the stone vault of the large hall.

"But since we are here, come and have a look at this." De Giorgis was pointing to a tall glassless arched window facing the coast and the mountains beyond.

"This is definitely a tower with a view," Bruno said, glancing outside. "I want to have a look at it from upstairs, too." He pointed to a little stone staircase in the opposite corner.

As he left, Giò approached De Giorgis. "I'm very sorry, sir."

"Sorry for what?"

With a beautifully engraved ancient dirk, Giò pretended to stab the man.

"Oh, Giò, not you." De Giorgis pressed his hands to his heart. "I would never have imagined you were the villain."

"Believe me when I say I would like to have killed someone else if I'd had a choice." She raised her eyebrows up on her forehead in a comically resigned expression. "But murderers often have their hands tied and little say in the choice of their victims."

"Is Bruno going to find me here?"

"No, he mustn't see you. You stay here, hidden by the wall, and I will tell him you decided to walk down to the pier. We'll be looking for you by lunchtime. Alessandra suggested we leave the knife and this jacket here," she said, removing a garment from her bag. "It has a copy of your ID and will act as a stand in for you. The weather wasn't supposed to be this bad when she first imagined the story. Once we're gone, you can walk back and shut yourself in your bedroom, but do not open the door, even when we come knocking, searching for you."

"OK, I'll wait for you and Bruno to be gone."

"At 11.30, we're starting the cookery lesson. That's when you can sneak in. It would be nice if you could come back here by 1pm, so that we can find you 'dead' instead of just the jacket. But the final decision on that is up to you – and the weather conditions, of course."

"I'll do the best a dead man can." He smiled at her as he hid away.

7

ISOLATED!

At 11 o'clock, as Bruno and Giò reached the villa, a shrill voice announced, "Time for our coffee break!"

The small party from the yoga class joined them in the living room where a few open sandwiches had been carefully laid out on a table. While they were eating and sipping their coffees, Filippa asked Giò and Bruno about De Giorgis.

"He said he isn't interested in the cookery lesson." Giò laughed, repeating his words. "His talent is only in the eating process."

"But maybe he wants to join us for coffee. I'll see if he's in the library," Marinella offered promptly. Ivo gave her a meaningful look, but she didn't acknowledge it.

When she came back into the living room a little while later, the others were still chattering, teasing Giò for her preference for long Americanos versus the local expresso.

But what satisfaction to hold a hot cup in my hands…

"He doesn't seem to be anywhere," Marinella announced, interrupting Giò's thoughts. "I even knocked on the door of his room."

Giò looked around to exchange a concerned glance with Alessandra, her partner in crime, but as she couldn't find her, she looked anxiously out of the window instead, fearing the man could come in right now and spoil the whole thing. But who could blame him if he decided to come back sooner than she'd asked? It looked likely to start raining at any moment.

Deep in thought, Giò made her way towards her room. As it was only 11.10, she had time to change her trousers for something more comfortable. Her short hair, ruffled by the wind, needed some serious combing – it would never tame her rebellious hair, but at least she could make it look somewhat less dishevelled.

She stopped by the side window, the one with the best view. The ocean's colour had turned to a deep grey, and some patches were almost black as the waters hurled and swelled, blurring the horizon. There was a special fascination in looking at the frenzied elements from a safe, comfortable distance.

Just beneath her other window, Giò noticed Ivo and Marinella moving around in the garden, almost certainly looking for the right spot for some more photos. Bianca and Caterina were also busy outside, and Bruno and Filippa had disappeared in the direction of the lighthouse. Should she join the others in the garden? Nope, she'd enjoy her free time, sitting in her armchair in front of the window. She had taken enough cold for one day.

When Giò went downstairs, she found her companions were still scattered all over the place. Marinella couldn't find her camera, the one she had used in the yoga room, so the whole party had been treasure hunting ever since Giò had left. They had searched inside and outside the house, as Marinella had taken a short walk in the garden after the yoga lesson.

As they all reconvened in the living room, Alessandra, slightly out of breath from the unplanned exercise, crashed onto the sofa, only to find the camera between the cushions.

"I never sat there," Marinella cried.

Alessandra rolled her eyes.

"Maybe someone was playing a trick on you." Bruno smiled as Marinella's eyes went straight to Filippa, who shrugged her shoulders indifferently.

"Giorgio isn't back yet," she said, shivering from her short walk outdoors.

"I suggest we move to the kitchen," Caterina said. "I'm sure Mr De Giorgis is enjoying a walk around the island, and there's plenty of refreshments left for his coffee break when he comes back. But let's hurry – it's 11.45 and my mum will be mad at me if we're any later as she needs time after the lesson to prepare the rest of our lunch."

"Bruno, you'll have to take a few pictures of me. There was no way I could convince Ivo to join us," Marinella announced as they entered the kitchen.

In reply, an unhappy grumble rose from the others.

"Well, this is my life as a blogger," Marinella snapped back. "I can't do as you all do, pretending to work while enjoying life. An influencer's career is much harder than that!"

"Whatever, as long as you watch your camera and spare me another 30 minutes of treasure hunting," Filippa said.

"You didn't exactly work yourself to death earlier on," Marinella replied fiercely, brandishing her rolling pin in the air.

WHEN THEY CAME OUT OF THE KITCHEN, THEY HAD TRACES OF FLOUR on their clothes and hair, and the satisfied expressions of people who had created something with their own hands.

"We'd better get changed before lunch." Filippa laughed as she looked at Bruno's floury hands – the ones that had horrified Marinella when he'd reached for her camera to take some photos for her. Caterina had volunteered to take his place as a photographer, and the poor misunderstood blogger had had to take her up on her offer, as unsatisfactory as it was.

"Ivo should take a look at these," Marinella cried, holding up her camera with the latest shots.

"I think he's still in the library," Caterina said.

"What time are we having lunch?"

"At 1.30. You have 30 minutes to freshen up and relax." Bianca continued to organise her guests and staff relentlessly. "It's been a full morning, and I think Alessandra will give you some clues after lunch."

"How thrilling!" Giò said.

"Help! Please help me!" Marinella cried from the library.

"Oh no! Someone else has been murdered before we've even had a chance to wash our hands," Bruno said, chuckling.

"Have they no respect?" Giò joined in with his laughter as they all went towards the library, teasing each other. But when the girlish scream rang out again, they increased their pace and entered the room to a shocking spectacle.

Ivo was sitting on an armchair. In front of him lay a newspaper, and his torso and head rested against the back of his seat. And from his breast, the handle of a knife protruded, a large stain of blood reddening his white shirt: the perfect representation of a murder in the library.

"Oh my goodness! You'll scare the life out of me, Alessandra," Filippa said.

"Ivo's going to steal your thunder as an actress," Bruno teased her. When Alessandra continued to look taken aback, he added, "You're acting again, aren't you? You won't fool us twice."

Marinella was staring at them, for once looking genuinely distraught. "Help, help, help!" she implored.

"Come on, we should be a bit more sympathetic," Giò said, moving towards Ivo. Something about his features gave her the impression all was not right with him, and when she touched him and felt the unnatural stillness of his body, she cried, "Oh my goodness, Bianca, call the hospital and the police!"

Alessandra, who was next to Giò, put her hand on Ivo's neck to feel for a pulse. "This is real. Caterina, take out the phones." Then she touched his chest and showed her fingers stained red. "He's dead! He's been killed!"

As weird and macabre as it seemed, both Caterina and Bruno came forward. They were not going to be convinced until they'd touched Ivo's lifeless body themselves.

Marinella was on her knees beside him, crying, "Why don't you help me? What are you waiting for?"

Caterina finally went to fetch the phones, while Bianca took Marinella to sit on the sofa and hugged her for comfort. Filippa was still standing in front of Ivo, her hand pressed to her mouth so hard that her lips were being cut against her teeth.

Giò went to stand beside her. "Don't worry, the police will be here soon."

"No they won't," Bruno replied, his face aghast. "The sea is too rough for them to reach the island."

CATERINA'S HEAD POPPED AROUND THE LIBRARY DOOR. "BIANCA, please could you come over here?"

Bianca left Marinella, asking Giò to take her place in comforting the girl. But Giò didn't make much headway before they all heard Bianca's voice, screaming from the corridor.

"What do you mean, they're gone?"

"Bruno, please go and see what has happened," Filippa said, her eyes still fixed on her former husband, unable to believe what had occurred. She tried to approach Marinella, but the latter shrank away like a wild animal caught in a trap.

"You awful woman! You killed him out of jealousy!"

"Marinella, dear, whatever are you saying?"

"You won't fool me with that innocent air. I know you hated him – you couldn't stand the fact that he'd found me, the love of his life. You wanted him to be concerned about you and only you."

"I know you are devastated, but I would never kill Ivo. I admit I was mad at him, but I wouldn't hurt him, not at all!"

"But you're going to inherit quite a bit of money now, aren't you?"

Filippa looked at Marinella, her mouth open, unable to utter a single syllable. An inscrutable expression crossed her face.

Is that the helpless look of the innocent who doesn't know how to prove she's not guilty? Or is it something else? Giò wondered

"You've been after his money ever since you split; you were afraid he'd finally divorce you to marry me, and you'd lose all of your claims on his money."

"I'd better leave this room before I say something I may regret, but there's no truth in what you're accusing me of," Filippa said, turning away and heading off in the direction of the living room.

Bruno came back a few minutes later. "You'd better join us in the living room," he said to Marinella and Giò, the only ones still in the library. "I will lock the door to the library. We need to try to make sense of what's happened."

"I want to stay here, close to him," Marinella cried.

"You can't stay here alone. Carmela has prepared some strong tea for you, and the rest of us. Come on, girl."

Supported by Bruno and Giò, Marinella reached the sofa in the living room. Bianca, Caterina and Alessandra arrived on the threshold from three different directions and exchanged a few worried words. Then Carmela came through from the kitchen with a pot of strong tea and mugs for all present.

"Please, take a seat." Bianca, paler than ever, pointed to the chairs and sofas. "Giorgio is not here yet," she added to Alessandra. "Would you knock on his door?"

"With all this chaos, why wouldn't he come down?" Filippa asked.

"He must have thought the screams and the noise were part of the game," Giò said.

"We will wait for him before getting started," Bianca said, pouring the tea into one of the mugs to make sure it was strong enough.

"There's no answer from his room," said Alessandra a short while later, coming back from upstairs. Bianca's brows moved upwards in dismay. Alessandra asked Giò, "Did you tell him not to reply to our knocks?"

"Yes, I followed your instructions."

"I can't understand why he won't answer," Filippa wondered.

"It's part of the game, he's meant to play dead," Giò muttered, almost hating herself for having to use those words.

"That's so perverse! I knew I would hate this murder weekend from the start!" Filippa cried.

Bianca spoke before anyone could respond with anything unpleasant. "Caterina, please take the second set of keys, knock on Giorgio's door and tell him the game has been interrupted due to an accident. If there's no reply, enter the room and find out what he is up to. His keys are the purple ones."

A few minutes later, Caterina was back, saying that the room was empty. Giò and Bruno went upstairs, as if checking in person could change the state of things. It was hard to tell if the man had come back at all after their morning walk.

Giò looked at Bruno. "Maybe he's gone back to the tower. I told him it would be more fun to find him there, but I didn't expect him to do it since the weather is so poor." She looked at the windowpanes, now being battered by a violent rainstorm.

"But why would he go out in this weather?" Bruno asked in surprise.

"Because that was our plan," Giò said.

The others looked at her without understanding. She instinctively looked at Bianca, as if she had to ask permission to reveal the game. Somehow the real murder... well, it still didn't seem that real.

With a silent nod of approval from Bianca, she explained. "In the game, I was supposed to be the villain, and I had murdered Mr De Giorgis in the Saracen Tower. I gave him the instructions that I'd received from Alessandra and asked him to hide while Bruno and I came back here. He said he would come back himself around 11.30 when we'd started the cookery class, and would go back to the tower before we'd finished so we could find him there. We left a jacket there as a stand in just in case he didn't feel like walking back. The jacket had some instructions from Alessandra in the pocket."

"So maybe he walked to the tower just before the lesson ended and was taken by surprise by the storm. He has shelter there, so as soon as it calms down, I'm going to look for him," Bruno concluded. They all nodded in relief.

"Bianca, have you contacted the police?" Filippa asked.

"That's why I wanted you all here," Bianca said. "Apparently the security box, with all the mobiles and the modem, has been taken."

"Taken?"

"Yes. I kept the locked box on the writing table in my own bedroom, but it's gone."

"You mean we have no way to communicate with the mainland?" Bruno asked.

Bianca shook her head.

"You don't have another phone or mobile?" Bruno insisted, waving his hands in agitation.

"We're on a small island," Bianca explained, "so we just have to rely on mobiles and the satellite for the internet connection. I had an emergency mobile in a drawer, but that's gone too."

"So we're completely isolated?" Giò gasped.

"We are."

8

MISSING OR GUILTY?

The storm was still raging when the clock chimed two. Everyone started, looking at each other.

"It's strange that Giorgio isn't here," Bianca said. "If he was expecting us to look for him after the cookery lesson, he'd surely be wondering why we haven't turned up yet."

"He probably thinks we haven't been looking for the same reason he hasn't come back: so as not to get drenched," Filippa replied.

"It takes less than ten minutes to reach the villa from the Saracen Tower," Giò said, unconvinced. "I'd rather get drenched and have a hot shower in a cosy room than stay dry in the cold for hours."

"You're right," Bruno mumbled. "Caterina, when did you clean De Giorgis's room?"

"When you went out for your walk. I cleaned Giò's first, then yours and his. I thought because of the weather that you might be finished before the folks in the yoga class."

"You were also in De Giorgis's room just now. Does it look as if he came back at all after the walk?"

"I'd say not. Everything seems to be as I left it, but I can't be sure."

"Has anybody seen him since Giò and I left the Saracen Tower?" Bruno asked, scanning all the people who were sitting in the living room. One by one, they shook their heads. Nobody, apart from Giò and Bruno, had seen De Giorgis since breakfast.

"You think that maybe he didn't come back at all?" ventured Giò.

"That's not really what I was thinking. Maybe he came back to the villa, but didn't return to his own room."

"Why wouldn't he go to his room if he came back? And where is he now?" Bianca asked.

"I don't like it, but I may have an answer to that," said Bruno, moving his gaze from Giò to Alessandra, then on to Bianca. "The first thing we need to do," he continued, "is to lock both the main door and the two balcony doors. If De Giorgis is still on the island and wants to get in, he will have to ring the bell then. We will also make a search throughout the house to ensure nobody else is inside, and while we are at it, we can look for the security box containing our mobiles."

"I can understand why we should search for the mobiles," Filippa said, looking him straight in the eyes, "but I can't see the point of locking the doors since it's just us on the island."

"If you allow me, I'd rather explain that later." Bruno had recovered his cool, giving orders as if he was coordinating one of his dangerous missions abroad. "Now let's divide into parties to search the house. Look under the beds and in the wardrobes; don't neglect any place where a person could hide."

Bianca opened her mouth as if she wanted to ask for more explanation, but then appeared to change her mind and went off to search with Giò and Filippa.

AFTER A THOROUGH SEARCH OF THE WHOLE HOUSE, ROOM BY ROOM, not forgetting the storerooms, cellar or attic, they had found no sign of De Giorgis or the mobile phones. When they all met up again downstairs, Bianca took back command of her home.

"Caterina and Carmela, could you prepare some food? We still need to eat, even if it's just a light sandwich."

"At least we know we're safe inside," said Bruno, sinking onto one of the armchairs.

"I don't understand what you're implying," snapped Bianca with an unusual display of temper.

"I will explain in a while, but after we've eaten something."

In a few minutes, Caterina and Carmela returned with two trays of sandwiches, which they laid out on the table close to the sofas. It was a rather silent meal, interrupted only by sobs from Marinella, who didn't seem to have lost her appetite despite her grief, and ate all her sandwiches. When the mugs were filled with coffee, Bianca finally addressed Bruno again, her voice firm and stable.

"So what's all this about?"

"I know you're a good friend of his, Bianca. And I grant you I held him in high esteem, even before I'd met him here. But frankly, one man has been killed, and another has mysteriously disappeared when a storm is raging outside. Instead of coming back here in search of shelter, he has decided to linger outside, we don't know where. Well, it can't merely be a coincidence, can it?"

His words lingered in the air for a few seconds. Bianca was dumbfounded, but could think of no counterarguments. All she could utter was one question, which only served to underline the implications of what Bruno had said.

"Why would Giorgio do something like this?"

Bruno had no time to reply.

"He killed him!" Marinella shouted, coming out of a semiconscious state caused by a combination of shock, headache and the painkillers' sleep-inducing effects. "Can't you see? De Giorgis has killed my Ivo – he has always hated him. Ivo told me to stay away from that man, but I didn't believe him. I thought

Ivo was simply jealous of De Giorgis's success, but he was right! The man is an unscrupulous killer."

"Did Ivo tell you something in particular?" Bruno asked, surprised that the girl's vehemence, turned on Filippa earlier, had switched so easily to De Giorgis.

"He said the man had ruined him in the past, that he'd be the head of a real newspaper if De Giorgis had not discredited him."

"But that's an old story," Filippa said, grateful that suspicion seemed to be turning away from her, but determined not to heap the same injustice on her friend. "It was actually Ivo's fault for being dodgy and writing libellous articles without checking his sources. Giorgio did his job properly and unmasked him. I know it's cruel to say it right now, but Ivo was no saint."

"I can't believe you're making accusations against him now that he's dead!"

"I'm not accusing him of anything, just repeating well-known facts. I was his wife at the time, remember?"

"I'm telling you, De Giorgis made it all up." Marinella stood up, moving around with exaggerated gestures like an actress on a stage. "And now, when he came face to face with Ivo, he decided to get rid of him. He hid our mobiles and ran away before we could raise the alarm."

Giò looked at the storm raging outside. "It would be madness to leave the island right now."

"Unless you have a good reason to do so," Bruno added. "But until midday, it wasn't so bad – rough, but not a real storm as it is now. I think De Giorgis might have killed Della Volpe as we left for the cookery class, then snatched our phones and fled."

"Do you think they argued, and in a rage..." Giò felt a sting in her heart. She had really admired De Giorgis.

"I don't know his reasons," Bruno admitted, "but yes, I believe De Giorgis killed Della Volpe, then hid our phones, or hurled them into the ocean, so we couldn't raise the alarm. If he's managed to reach land, all he has to do is to fly from country to country until the police lose track of him. Some countries are happy to welcome wealthy criminals."

"But he won't be able to transfer his money today or tomorrow," Giò said.

"Unless—" Bruno paused in order to capture the full attention of the others "—he's already planned ahead."

"In which case," Alessandra said slowly, "it was premeditated murder."

"That's what I suspect. Anyway, how is the weather doing? We can't stay on this island forever."

"By late tomorrow morning, the sea should have calmed down," Caterina replied. "I checked the weather forecasts last night."

They all looked at her gratefully. Just one more day and they could leave this place.

"We'll wait for the storm to cool down a little," said Bruno, nodding, "then I'd like to search the island. We need to know if that man is still here or if he's really gone. In the meantime, let's go over what we know. When did we last see Della Volpe?"

"Well, I guess when he retired to the library," Alessandra said, "just after we found Marinella's camera and went in for the cookery class."

"But there were people who came along later or left the class for a while..." Bruno looked at Filippa.

"That's true. I didn't need my glasses for yoga, but I wanted them to take notes during the masterclass and to make sure I used the right ingredients in the right amounts."

"Exactly, so did you see Ivo?"

"Only briefly. I actually wanted to check to see if Giorgio had come back at all. I had an impression he wanted to tell me something this morning, but we never had the time."

As Filippa said this, Giò remembered the man knocking on her door the night before.

Filippa continued, "After I'd fetched my glasses, I popped into the library. Ivo was already sitting there, reading the newspaper, but there was no trace of Giorgio, so I simply left. I don't think Ivo even noticed me."

"Was Ivo alone in the room?"

"Yes, definitely."

"Was he alive?"

"Oh my goodness, he certainly was. I would have noticed had he been as we found him." And her mind pictured him with his arms unfolded, reclining back onto the chair, his injured chest in full view.

"But he wasn't in that position when I went in." Marinella tried in vain to gulp back her tears. "He was sitting on the chair, seemingly reading his newspaper. I called to him and he didn't reply, but I thought he was joking. Then I shook him and he fell back on the chair, and that's when I saw the knife and knew he was dead."

"Oh my!" Bianca cried.

"Give it some more thought, Filippa," Bruno continued, dispassionately. "Have you any idea if he was alive or not when you peered into the library? Maybe he was already in the position that Marinella found him in."

"I think he was fine. That is…" Filippa seemed at a loss for words, probably concerned about returning to the top of the suspects list again "…that's what I thought at the time. I didn't look too closely at him – I was searching for Giorgio, and I didn't want to speak to Ivo if I could avoid it…"

Bruno cut her short and moved on. "Did anybody else go into the library after Filippa?"

They all shook their heads, stopping as the clock chimed 3pm.

It was again Bruno's voice that broke the silence.

"We need to go and check if the boat is still here. I do believe the storm has weakened momentarily."

9

ONE OF US

"Whoever goes to search had better go in a party of at least three," said Bianca.

Giò, Caterina and Bruno volunteered to go. They wanted to ascertain whether the boat had been used by De Giorgis to escape from the island while the storm had lulled.

"Please do not under any circumstances behave stupidly like the heroes in books," Alessandra added. "Stick together all the time."

At the harbour, the three explorers found to their surprise that the boat was still moored up.

"I was sure we were going to discover it had gone," said Bruno.

"I'm relieved that tomorrow we should be able to leave the island…"

"I'm not sure I feel better," Giò said. "Does this mean De Giorgis is still on the island? He must be out of his mind to spend all this time outside in these weather conditions?"

Caterina asked the other two to hold the boat stable while she took a closer look. She marched all the way to the cockpit, then turned towards the stern to examine the engine.

"We won't be able to use the boat after all," she said. "The electric cables to the engine have been chopped to pieces!"

"My goodness," cried Bruno in shock, "the man is still here and he doesn't want us to leave the island. Did the others lock the door after we left?"

"Yes, I told them to do so," Giò said.

"Could De Giorgis have left the island any other way?"

"There are the kayaks. In fact," said Caterina, peering at the kayaks piled up in the covered shelter, "one is missing."

"Why would he use a kayak and not the boat?" wondered Giò, more to herself than anyone else, but Caterina felt compelled to attempt to answer.

"It's madness to try and leave in anything in this weather. The explanation might be that you have to know your way out with the boat because of the rocks just beneath the surface. Maybe he felt safer in the kayak, though it's still pure folly."

"Shall we go back to the ruins of the tower and check there?" Bruno asked his companions.

"We've no weapons on us," Caterina murmured. "And the man might be dangerous."

"I'm not sure I'll feel better tonight," said Giò, "knowing he could break into the house at any moment, under cover of darkness."

Bruno and Caterina nodded in agreement.

As the tower came into view, Giò's heart went pitter-pat.

"Watch out for any movement, anything out of place," said Bruno. "I'll go inside first. If you see me assaulted, just run away back to the guesthouse. Don't play the heroines. He's not the man we thought we knew."

Going inside the tower, he moved like he had been taught during his military training a long time ago, skills that had already proved useful when he travelled through difficult countries or regions in wartime. But this time there was no danger: the tower was empty.

"Nobody inside," he reassured the women. "You have a look around the outside, proceeding in opposite directions, and I'll explore upstairs. If you see anything, don't think, just shout as loud as you can."

Giò went round the southern part of the ruins, her eyes scanning each detail: the tower walls, the little grassy space around them, the boulders from behind which De Giorgis could ambush her at any time. Finally she spotted Bruno in one of the arched windows and waved to him.

Caterina arrived from the opposite direction, shaking her head. "He isn't out here, either."

Bruno came down and joined them. "Shall we have a look at the lighthouse too?" he asked.

"But even if he broke in," Caterina said, "it's just the stairs and the lantern room, no other floors. He certainly can't plan to spend the night there."

"I agree," said Giò. "Either our man has already left the island, or he'll try to break into the house this evening."

Bruno pointed to the path going towards the lighthouse. "All the same, I'd feel better if we had a look there too."

Caterina stopped him. "Certainly not along the path," she said. "It's too exposed, and the wind is even stronger than it was this morning. We'll have to use the main road. It takes a bit longer, but it's infinitely safer."

"And passing by the villa, we could tell the others about the boat and the kayak, and warn them to be extra careful," added Giò.

They walked to where the gravel road branched. On the right, it went up towards the exposed rock path that Giò had hiked along that morning with Bruno and De Giorgis; on the left, it led towards the road. Giò paused. Thunder the cat was sitting on a boulder in the belvedere, looking down at the wild sea. She slowly reached out for him, keeping her distance so as not to disturb him. The cat fixed his shining green eyes on her, but he didn't leave – the woman seemed to be the inoffensive kind. As for Giò, she was not only attracted to the elusive cat, but also curious to see what had caught his attention. She followed his gaze and a loud cry left her lips.

"And what's that?" Her index finger pointed to a small red mass at the bottom of the rocky wall, floating to the rhythm of the waves. As Thunder meowed and sprang away, disturbed by the loud intruder, the other two joined her and looked in the direction her finger was pointing.

"That looks like De Giorgis's rain jacket," Caterina yelled. "It's his body, being battered by the waves."

"I can't see the kayak, but it looks as if his attempt to leave the island was not a successful one," Bruno concluded sardonically.

"Oh my goodness, will we be able to fetch his body?" Giò asked.

"Nope." Caterina shook her head. "It would be almost impossible in good weather to get down there, except by sea. Right now on the slippery rocks, it would be suicide..." She paused meaningfully on the last word.

"He's lying face down in the water." Bruno tried to soothe the shocked Giò. "Believe me, he's been dead for a long time."

"The ocean is so violent," Giò said, burying her face in her hands, "the rescue team will find nothing but his bones by tomorrow."

"And then there were bones," Bruno whispered gloomily.

They kept looking at the figure being shoved against the rocks by the restless waves for a while until the rain started again. The rain and wind combined made conversation impossible once more, pushing their words back down their throats.

What a strange mix of feelings, thought Giò as they headed towards the guesthouse. The whole weekend, intended to be so much fun, had taken a tragic turn. At the same time, she felt pity for De Giorgis, for the madness that had fallen on him, along with an undeniable sense of relief, her survival instinct crying out that at least they were safe.

∼

WHEN THEY REACHED THE VILLA, THEY FOUND ALL THE OTHERS STILL assembled in the living room. Bruno told them about the boat, the kayak, and finally the body floating in the water.

"I told you he was completely mad, but why did he kill my Ivo?" Marinella was clearly back to her usual self. There was something so overly tragic about her appearance, it seemed she was rehearsing for her next YouTube video. With such a story to tell upon her return to the online world, she would see her hits skyrocket, no doubt.

As comments and exclamations of surprise filled the room, Bianca whispered to Giò, "Carmela looks a bit tired and stressed out. I want to give her a break." Then in a louder voice, she said, "Giò and I are going to prepare some strong tea for everyone."

Giò followed her into the kitchen. Bianca wore a thoughtful expression.

"There's something wrong here. I've known Giorgio for years and I can't believe he did what you're all saying he did. And why would he? I didn't want to speak my mind in front of Marinella or Filippa, but Ivo and Giorgio were at either end of the spectrum in terms of morals."

Giò tried to comfort her friend. "We don't know what happened exactly."

"But it's not like him at all. I really couldn't believe what Bruno said when we found Ivo, but now that we've found out that Giorgio is dead, too... No, Giò, I can tell you, it's not what it looks like."

"OK, OK, don't distress yourself. Tomorrow the police are coming and they will be able to make sense of all this."

Bianca looked Giò in the eyes. "I feel guilty. I wish I had never started this. It was such a silly idea."

"Of course it wasn't, and you should know by now how guilt works: it claims more victims among the innocent than those who are actually responsible."

Bianca finally smiled. "You're right, Giò. There are two kinds of people: those who think they are always in the right even when they're not, and those who feel guilty when they shouldn't."

"And we're both stupid enough to belong to the second group." Giò gave Bianca a comforting hug, followed by a little laughter from both women. "But we need to learn to take only our fair share of guilt, no more, don't we?"

"I promise I'll try," Bianca replied. "Let's join the others, and take a tray of tea and coffee with us."

BIANCA WAS ABOUT TO FILL FILIPPA'S CUP WITH HOT TEA WHEN SHE stopped, the teapot poised in mid-air.

"It can't be!" she yelled.

"What?" asked Filippa, still holding up her cup.

"It simply can't be." Ignoring Filippa's cup, Bianca put the teapot down on the table and marched determinedly to her study.

A few minutes later, she came back with a map in her hands which she laid on the table to show the others.

"Today's wind started from north-northwest and moved to south-southeast," she said, her hand tracing imaginary lines on the map as she talked. "There's no way Giorgio and his kayak could have exited the pier in the south and reached the inlet beneath the Saracen Tower, which is in the northern part of the island. Had he been so mad as to venture out on the sea in a kayak, the currents would have taken him directly towards the southern coastline, not all around the island…

backwards, if you see what I mean." Her finger traced an abrupt turn.

"But the body we saw, it's De Giorgis," Caterina said.

"I don't doubt it, but he must have fallen from the cliffs…"

"He killed himself," Marinella said, interrupting Bianca's words and making the sign of the cross. "After he murdered my Ivo, he realised his madness, went to the rocky cliffs and launched himself into the abyss."

"Nonsense! Giorgio has always taken responsibility for his actions, and besides, he's not the type of person who would kill himself," Bianca said with a newfound confidence.

"You never know what can go wrong in the human mind," Filippa whispered.

"It can't be that!" Giò looked at Filippa through narrowed eyes, her suspicions aroused again. "The killer didn't act on impulse. He, or she, has designed the whole thing well. Do you remember? He – or she – also took away all our mobiles and the modem. He doesn't want us to communicate with the mainland so he can buy himself time."

"Then what happened to Giorgio if he didn't kill himself?" asked Filippa, although like the rest of those present, by now she could guess the reply.

"Someone pushed him!" Bianca said without hesitation.

"And after having killed Giorgio and Ivo, the killer got in the kayak and left the island?" asked Caterina.

"Of course not, nobody left in the kayak," Giò replied.

"But someone took one."

"That's what the killer wants us to think. The villain killed De Giorgis, then Ivo, or maybe in the opposite order, we don't really know. When he went to cut the boat engine cables, he was struck with the idea of leaving a kayak in the water. If De Giorgis's corpse had not been trapped by the rocks, it would have reached the coast along with the kayak. We would have assumed that De Giorgis had tried to flee the island, but lost control of the kayak and the two ended up at different points along the coast."

"But if the killer has not left the island… it means he or she is still here," Filippa cried, raking her hair beneath her ear with a shaky hand.

"Exactly."

"In this room?"

Giò decided it was time to voice that truth. "Yes, he or she is here in this room. The murderer is one of us."

10

A CRUEL EXERCISE

The silence that followed the revelation was broken by Giò, who spoke in an unusually soft voice as if talking to herself.

"But why? Why this double homicide? Who might have a reason to do that? What associates Ivo's death with Mr De Giorgis's?"

"I would understand someone wanting De Giorgis dead," Bruno continued from where Giò's thoughts had halted. "He was a rather uncomfortable man to be around, able to recognise the truth where no one else could spot it. He had strong ethics, and maybe he knew something damning about one of us. Della Volpe was a totally different kind of chap. I could imagine someone wanting to kill him too, but for totally different reasons. He could easily stir up hatred by being so full of himself, and sometimes he humiliated people. But I can't see why any one person would want to kill two people as different as those two. They've never run a special report or investigation together, as far as I know."

"Are you suggesting Ivo deserved to die more than De Giorgis?" snapped Marinella, banging the cup she was holding on the table.

"Marinella, bear with me." Bruno smiled at her almost tenderly. "I know it's hard, but since the killer is here, and we have no idea about their intentions, we'll have to do without the normal politeness society expects from us on the occasion of the death of a loved one. What I'm trying to say is that I can't imagine the killer murdered those two men for the same reason. And we need to understand what this is all about…"

"I say that the police will be here tomorrow afternoon at the latest," Bianca interrupted Bruno, fearing the consequences if he were to carry on airing his train of thought. "It's up to them to find out the truth. We shouldn't play the sleuths."

"I wish it was as simple as that." Bruno shook his head. "But what if the killer hasn't accomplished his mission yet? What if he has to kill someone else before the police get here tomorrow?"

"How can you suggest that?" Filippa looked at him, horrified, but Bruno carried on relentlessly.

"He's killed twice. If we ignore his motives, why should he stop at two?"

"You don't mean it's like the book?" Marinella cried, real terror seizing her this time. "The killer wants to kill all of us, as in Agatha Christie's story?"

"That would make no sense, unless under her calm appearance, Bianca is a maniac who has decided to end her career on this island with a dastardly deed that would go down in history. Maybe the things that voice accused us of, the things that we thought were jokes, are in fact true. Maybe she has found us all guilty and wants to repeat the *And Then There Were None* experiment."

Bruno smiled at his own absurdity, but the others all looked up at Bianca, who shrugged.

"It's very difficult to demonstrate the insanity of such an accusation, so I won't even try." Her tone was angry, but maybe she could see the point behind Bruno's words.

"Giò and I were the last to see De Giorgis alive at the Saracen Tower," Bruno continued. "None of us crossed his path after we came back. And again, none of us, apart from Filippa, has admitted seeing Della Volpe once he left for the library after the coffee break, before the cookery class. Did Bianca have the time to go to the tower unseen? As I remember, she arrived for the cookery lesson a little later than the rest of us, so I'd say yes, she had the time. Did she also have the time to kill Della Volpe? Yes, that was even easier."

Bianca, though red in the face, nodded as Bruno continued.

"Alessandra, you were the one who actually wrote the story and accusations, so maybe you did a little digging into our lives. We know so very little about you – we didn't even know you were from Russia until you spoke to De Giorgis. Maybe you're a madwoman, determined to leave a mark in the criminal history record books with a recreation of Agatha Christie's story. After all, you're an artist. Folly and talent often come intertwined. Did you have an opportunity? Of course. You were outside for a long while during the coffee break, looking for Marinella's camera, then with the excuse of having to change your wet clothes, you also joined the class a little later."

"Are you going to go over your own movements as well?" was Alessandra's cold reply.

"Of course, I have to. As for my motive, that's for you to find out. Maybe I'm a simple journalist obsessed with the greater fame of the other two. In that case, you'd be safe. I've killed my rivals, and I need not spill any more blood."

"Or maybe it's a trap so that we lower our guard," Caterina said, looking at Bruno as if for the first time. It was incredible how all of them were now looking at each other with suspicion, even those people who had instinctively trusted each other minutes before.

"Correct. Any of us, myself included, might be a maniac determined to bring the concept of justice to its extremes. As for the opportunity, of course Giò and I were both at the Saracen Tower with De Giorgis, so we each had a good opportunity to do him in, there and then. Also, I could have slipped into the library as soon as Della Volpe had settled in there and joined the others in perfect time for the class. A bit risky, but effective."

"Carmela never left the kitchen," Filippa said. "She might have killed Ivo, before or after the class, but she certainly didn't have enough time to run to the Saracen Tower and back."

"That's partly true," Bruno said placidly. "But Caterina had all the time she needed to kill De Giorgis, and the two may be acting together. Also, Carmela has a certain helpful skill – she knows how to use a knife."

Carmela didn't speak, but the reference to the knife made her cheeks turn crimson.

"This game is cruel, Bruno," said Filippa, anticipating his next words. "I could be just as guilty as all the others – I left the kitchen during the cookery class to fetch my glasses from upstairs, took a painkiller and spent a good 10 minutes lying on my bed before returning to the class. But as far as you know, I might have gone to the Saracen Tower to kill Giorgio, and then killed Ivo on the way back. Besides, I knew them both prior to this stay, so *I might have personal reasons for murdering them*," she said, and she stressed the last words.

"I'm sure it's the same with Marinella," Filippa continued. "She went outside during the coffee break to search for her camera, but maybe she ran to the tower instead. She could have killed Ivo when she pretended to have found him dead." She silenced the girl who was about to voice her protests. "Hold on, this is a zero sum game. We aren't excluding anybody. We could all have a motive, as mad as it may sound, and an opportunity. I can't see the point of torturing us anymore."

"You're right," Bruno agreed. "My intention was to see if any of us could be excluded, at least in terms of opportunity. But as it seems we cannot exclude anyone, I agree, it's a pointlessly cruel exercise."

"So where do we go from here?" Giò asked. "We can't just wait to see if the killer will strike again."

"Caterina, you said the storm and the sea will be quieter

tomorrow. Is there any way to repair the boat?" Alessandra asked.

Caterina shook her head. "Nope, the cables can't be fixed with what we've got. We can use the signal flares on the boat to alert the people in Praia a Mare, hoping someone on the coast will notice them. Tomorrow, as soon as the sea calms down, I could reach land with one of the kayaks and raise the alarm."

"I could come with you," said Bruno.

"I know where the rocks are and how the currents work. I normally organise kayak tours along the coast and to the island, but I'd be better going alone. But I'm no hero, so it all depends on the weather conditions."

"What if you run away?" Marinella asked suspiciously.

"If I'm the killer, you'll be better off without me. Certainly you won't starve on the island, and by Monday morning at the latest, people will wonder why nobody has come back to the mainland. They will try to contact Bianca, and when they find out all connections have been cut, they will raise the alarm for sure – if they haven't already. Our families, for all we know, might already be worried and concerned. We have no idea what's going on beyond the island."

"WHAT'S THE TIME?" MARINELLA ASKED FROM THE SOFA WHERE she'd been sitting for far too long.

"Half past five," Bianca replied wearily.

"My goodness, time is so slow," Filippa said. "Are we allowed to go to our rooms? I wouldn't mind resting a little."

"I'd advise against it," Bruno warned. He had been pretending to read a newspaper from the day before, but he had just been turning the pages aimlessly.

"Why?"

"While we are all together, no one can harm anyone else. You know how it is in books – the moment someone is alone, he or she is the most vulnerable."

"We'll have to go to bed at some point," Giò said, half yawning. She was not used to so much inactivity.

"Why?" Bruno asked. "In order to save my life, I'm more than happy to hang around here and give up a night's sleep."

"It will be a long night, but I believe it's the best thing to do, stick together," Alessandra agreed.

Instantly, Marinella protested. "We might need to go to the toilet or our room. I'd love to change into something more comfortable for the night and pick up a blanket from my room, it feels so cold."

"I think we can leave the group provided it's one at a time," Bruno reassured her, "but only for short breaks."

"It makes no sense. Do we really believe a maniac wants to kill us all?" Filippa said, hoping her words would expel her fears. "He's rather behind on his agenda if he's only got till midday tomorrow."

"Frankly, we don't know," Bruno replied. "But we'd better take all necessary precautions just in case." He was familiar with danger, and now that De Giorgis had gone, he was possibly the only one who could take responsibility for the safety of them all.

Again, an uneasy silence fell on the room, and it took a long while before the pendulum clock struck six.

"Only 6pm. My goodness, it will be torture to wait all night at this rate." Giò rose from her armchair and walked around the room. "I'm starting to believe I can hear noises from the other parts of the house."

"It's just the wind and the rain battering against the windows," Bianca reassured her. "But it's true, time never passes quickly when you're watching the clock. Anyone like to play cards?"

Marinella, Bruno and Caterina joined in, happy to have something else to occupy their minds. Giò had always hated card games.

"I'll choose a book from the shelves." Giò regretted she couldn't peruse the selection in the library, but she'd have to be happy with the few classics on the mantelpiece.

Pride and Prejudice *will do, though I know it by heart,* she thought as she started on page one.

Alessandra and Filippa chatted with Caterina's mum. At 7pm, Carmela asked, "Shall I go to the kitchen to prepare something for dinner? Could Caterina accompany me?"

"Of course not, imagine if you two wanted to poison us?" Marinella cried from the card table.

"They could have done it on Friday night," Bianca replied angrily, "as well as at breakfast this morning, and be done with all of us at once."

Marinella shook her head stubbornly. "But that's not how the story goes. We have to die one by one, with suspicion rolling from one person to the next."

"I'm starving, and some food will help us to pass the time," Alessandra said. "How about each of us goes to the kitchen one by one to fetch ourselves a sandwich?"

"Or how about splitting into two groups of four?" added Giò. "Four can go to the kitchen now to prepare dinner, the other four later to do the washing up. We'll sit down for a proper meal, and we might end up passing a couple of hours at least without going insane."

All hands went up, accepting Giò's proposal.

11

WAITING FOR DAWN

Between a few forced laughs and some chat, dinner passed pleasantly enough. The tension had apparently relaxed a little, although they all took precautions, opening only sealed ingredients and wine bottles.

By nine o'clock, they were in the living room again. Marinella asked if she could be the first one to go to her bedroom to freshen up and get ready for the night.

"I will go second," Filippa said as the girl went upstairs. "I'm already feeling drowsy, so I shouldn't have drunk any wine. I hope you will all be more vigilant than I may be."

"I think we can take it in turns to sleep." Bruno felt as if he was organising a camp in the middle of a desert or savannah. "Four keep watch, four try to sleep on the sofas."

It was then that the lights went out.

"Oh, my goodness!"

"What the devil?"

"It sometimes happens during a storm, the electricity gets cut off." Caterina's voice didn't sound as convincing as she'd hoped.

"What now?"

"My goodness, it's the killer!"

Marinella shrieked with all her strength from upstairs.

"Help! Help!"

Bruno cursed. "Do you have a torch anywhere, Bianca?"

"Yes, I'm looking for it. What are they doing to Marinella?" The girl was still screaming.

"If she's screaming, she's fine," Alessandra replied coldly.

"Caterina, dear, do you have any idea where the torch is? I'm standing by the cupboard."

"I'm coming, it should be in the left drawer." A flash of lightning illuminated the room for two to three seconds, enough for Bianca to spot the torch in the drawer.

"There it is! Are you all OK?" she said, shining the light around the room, counting everyone. "Seven including me. Marinella, you're by yourself," she called. "You should be fine."

The girl had reached the banisters. "I hate this place, I want to go home. What's happened? Why are the lights off?"

"It's the storm." Bianca pointed the torch towards the stairs so Marinella could come down without falling. "Are you OK?"

"We'll all be dead by tomorrow! We'll all be dead!"

"No, we won't. Come here."

"Do you have any candles?" Bruno asked.

"There are some in the kitchen," Caterina said, "but I need the torch to fetch them."

"I'm not going to wait in the dark," Alessandra said.

"We should also check the electric generator," Bianca suggested.

"Please, let's not split up."

"Do you have enough batteries for the torch to stay on all night?"

"I didn't check if there were more in the drawer."

With a few blinks, the lights came back on. A general sigh of relief crossed the room, but when the group scanned each other's faces, they were still dark with terror.

"We're all... ehm... OK," Bruno said, dismissing the word *alive* that had almost made its way to his lips, "aren't we?"

"We are, but I'm not going to survive another blackout," Giò said bluntly.

"That's what we all feel," Caterina said. "I guess we need a different arrangement for the night."

"First of all," Carmela said, "I'm going to check to see if there are more torches or candles."

"Please, bring all you find," said Bianca.

"She's going to hide them if she's the killer and say there's nothing in the house."

"You're right, Alessandra," said Bruno. "They've already taken away our mobiles and boat, let's not make the same mistake with the torches. Four people wait here, four check with Carmela for torches and candles. Bianca and Caterina, you'd better join the second group as you know the house as well as she does."

When the four came back, their findings didn't amount to much.

"We've got a packet of ten candles, plenty of matches, one small torch," Caterina announced.

"Should the lights go off again overnight," Giò said, "we won't have much to keep our spirits up. We don't even know if it was a trick played by the killer."

"We were all here," Bianca replied. "And even if the killer caused a short circuit to make the lights go off, he certainly couldn't have switched them back on again."

"Maybe you're right," Giò admitted. "But there aren't too many things I feel sure of right now."

"I'm sure I don't want to go through another blackout here in the company of a killer," Marinella added. "Especially since we don't have enough candles or torches to illuminate the whole room."

"I'd rather spend the night in my room," Filippa agreed with Marinella for once. "If we all lock ourselves in, we should be fine. Otherwise we'll become hysterical very shortly. The more I think about it, the more I believe De Giorgis killed Della Volpe and then took his own life. The other story is the fruit of our overactive imaginations, and we might cause an accident through fear if we're not careful."

"I still believe we should stick together for our own safety," Bruno said. "But of course, I'm not the one in charge. And certainly the possibility of blackouts changes things somewhat. Shall we vote?"

Only Bruno and Alessandra voted to spend the night all together in the living room; the others wanted to return to their own bedrooms.

"Majority wins," Bruno said sportingly. "We'll spend the night in our rooms, but by way of a precaution, I'm begging you not to leave your bedrooms till an agreed time tomorrow. We will come down all together at 8.30am. Under no circumstance should you venture out of your rooms before that. If the lights go off, just stay where you are. There's nothing much we can do about it, anyway. If someone knocks on your door, do not open it, unless you're certain there are at least three people outside. Finally, shout out as loud as you can if you hear any strange noises."

"We should also get our duplicate keys," suggested Alessandra.

"What's that?" Giò asked.

"Alessandra is right," Bianca explained. "Each room has a double set of keys. They are helpful for cleaning the rooms, when two guests share a room, or simply in case one is lost. We don't have a master key."

"I will fetch them," Alessandra said.

On her return, she distributed the keys to the relevant people according to a coloured ring attached to each one.

"I'd rather go now, I'm exhausted," Filippa said, passing a hand over her forehead.

There was a powerful crash of thunder outside. The lights flickered again, but stayed on.

"I'd say we'd all better go before there's another blackout," said Giò in a small voice. The others agreed.

"Caterina and Carmela, tomorrow at 8.30, come knocking at our doors so that we can all come out together." The mother and daughter had their bedrooms downstairs, so the rest of them left for the first floor.

Filippa was so sleepy that she jiggled her keys, trying in vain to insert one into the lock. In the end, Alessandra had to help her out.

Before leaving for the other wing, Marinella said tremulously, "I wish I could trust one of you to share my room, but it's better to stay alone."

Giò made sure she closed her door properly, leaving the key in the lock half turned so that nobody could try to get in with another key. She couldn't resist the temptation to pull the chest of drawers in front of the door as an added precaution. Then she locked her shutters and got changed, wishing she had her phone with her so she could listen to some music. As it was a retreat, the rooms in the guesthouse had no TV, and she regretted not having something silly and light-hearted to watch. She would have stayed awake in front of the TV and let the night pass her by.

She picked up the copy of *Pride and Prejudice* she'd brought up from the living room, but her thoughts soon drifted off to what was happening in the house. She thought about what Bruno had said.

"Who would want to kill two men as different as De Giorgis and Della Volpe?"

There had to be a thread linking the lives of the two men, but none of them had been able to see the connection. What were the killer's motives? Or were they really dealing with a serial killer? Maybe a fanatical Agatha Christie enthusiast was determined to make her novel come true.

Giò thought about each of the guests staying on the island one by one. Could she imagine any of them being a killer?

"You don't get to know a person in a lifetime," her gran would have said. *Imagine thinking I could know them after spending only one and a half days together.* She felt she could exclude Bianca, though how convenient it would have been for her, as the owner, to organise the whole thing. Easy to organise, but also easy to get caught. In the police's eyes, she'd be the first suspect.

But what about the others? Did the killer, whoever it was, really stand a chance of hiding their motives and evidence of their crimes once the police arrived? Unless the murderer was determined to kill them all before the police could reach the island, then kill him or herself too. Giò's rational mind had rejected this link to the *And Then There Were None* storyline earlier on, but now, with the raging thunderstorm outside and the lights blinking, she felt less sure.

But what was that? Was it a door opening? Were those footsteps that she heard, or was it just her overactive imagination?

She knocked gently on the wall separating her room from Filippa's. There was no reply – maybe Filippa was already sleeping. Or had she left her room, despite Bruno's recommendations? Why would anyone want to leave the safety of their room?

Had they dismissed the idea that Filippa could be the murderer too soon? After all, Marinella had told them all about the inheritance the woman stood to receive on Ivo's death, so she had a good motive to want to kill at least one of the victims. Had she gone to carry on with her mission? But if it was the inheritance she was after, why kill anyone else?

A few minutes later, Giò heard footsteps returning and the sound of a door being shut gently. Again she tapped on the wall, but there was still no answer.

Those few minutes had been enough for the killer to have forced someone's door open and claim one more victim. Should she have shouted and raised the alarm? Or was she reading too much into it?

All had gone quiet again within the building. Only the wind was still howling outside, accompanying Giò's thoughts which were hammering her brain with such force that she felt suddenly exhausted. She positioned her matches and candles on her bedside table, leaving the lamp on, and succumbed to a strange sleep, flavoured with fear.

PART III

SUNDAY

12

ON THE CLIFFS

When Giò woke up, daylight was filtering in through the shutters. She opened them and the sunlight entered the room, dispersing any malignant shadow of fear that may have been lingering. Although the sky was blue again, the air was coldish for June, but she inhaled it deeply, hoping it would clear her thoughts and the anxieties of the previous night.

Watching the indigo sea swelling beyond the holly forest, for a long moment, she felt as if she might have imagined it all: nobody had been murdered on this island of wild beauty. But when her eyes fell on the chest of drawers in front of the door, she knew it was all too real. Fortunately, the police would be here in a short time and the nightmare would be dealt with properly, and most importantly of all, she was still alive.

It was 7.30; she took a hot shower and got ready to join the others, impatient to see if the night had passed uneventfully for all of them too. At 8.20, Caterina and her mum knocked on her door.

"Coming!" Giò replied. Moving the chest of drawers, she then wondered if she should open her door as she heard the mother and daughter knocking for Filippa and Alessandra.

Caterina announced, "We're going to the other wing to call for the others."

Only when she heard them going did Giò open her door. The corridor was deserted, so she knocked on the other two rooms. There was no answer from Filippa, but Alessandra put her head round her door, her face tired, her brown eyes looking at Giò uncertainly as if she was undecided whether to step out or stay safely in her shelter.

Bianca appeared from the other wing. "We're almost ready here, only Marinella is finishing her beauty routine. Let's wait for her and all walk down together. Did you get any sleep, Giò?"

"Sort of," she replied.

Alessandra, her head still peering out from her bedroom, finally spoke. "Good morning, Giò, Bianca, I need two more minutes. Just a touch of lipstick – it may sound silly, but I know I look awful this morning. I'm so glad the night is over."

Bianca smiled at her. "Of course, Alessandra, we're a little ahead of time. I just can't wait to make sure everyone's fine."

Alessandra's head vanished into her room and Giò knocked again, this time with more force, on Filippa's door. Bianca, startled by the loud bangs, moved closer to Giò as Bruno and Caterina joined them.

"No answer from Filippa," Giò explained.

Bruno stood next to her and hammered on Filippa's door. It was impossible for her not to hear the banging. But no answer came from inside.

"Has she gone somewhere? Did you see anybody downstairs?" Bianca asked Caterina.

"I didn't check to see if the main door was unlocked, nor did I go into the library, but she certainly wasn't in the kitchen or living room."

"Please check to see if she's somewhere out in the garden."

"What's happening? I heard you banging on Filippa's door," Alessandra said, reappearing at her bedroom door. Wearing her trademark fiery red lipstick and plenty of mascara, she looked more like her usual self than she had minutes before.

"She's not answering," Giò explained. "I think I heard her going out in the middle of the night... Did you hear her at all?"

"No, I didn't," Alessandra replied. "I took a long, hot bath, then I went to bed, but I had my earphones on. Luckily my music is on my iPod rather than my phone."

Caterina returned. "The main door is locked, Filippa's balcony shutters are still closed, and she's nowhere else in the house. I've checked *all* rooms downstairs."

"Then we'll have to force this door. Bianca, you did say you don't have a master key, didn't you?" Bruno asked.

"No, no master key. We need to break in."

Marinella looked at her doubtfully. "Or maybe you have one, but how convenient to say you don't."

Bianca sent her a scornful glance. "Let's force this door."

To Giò's surprise, Bruno didn't even try to barge the door using his shoulder as she'd seen done in the movies; he simply kicked it with his foot at lock level until it gave in. Then he entered the room, and the others followed closely behind.

Filippa was lying on her bed; was she still asleep after all that banging? But something about the blankness of her expression looked unnatural. Then they noticed, touched by the fingertips of her right hand, cast aside on the duvet, a gun. And on the side of her forehead facing the window was a gunshot wound.

"She's killed herself!" Bianca shouted.

"My goodness," Alessandra cried, covering her pale face with her hands. Marinella fainted, and Giò and Bruno took her into Giò's bedroom while Caterina prepared some water and sugar using the tea things laid out in there. As the girl came back to her senses, Bruno returned to Filippa's room, and Giò, despite herself, followed on behind.

"We shouldn't touch anything," said Bruno, looking closely at Filippa's wound, her hand position, the gun. On the bedside table were a few sleeping pills. "I think these helped her to find the courage for this extreme gesture."

"But why?" cried Bianca.

"The tension? The fear, maybe?"

Bruno bent down to examine the bedside table. Next to the pills was a large dish that had been used to burn a few pieces of paper, a box of matches nearby.

"Or maybe it was for a totally different reason…"

On one of the less burnt fragments, he read aloud, *"The inheritance might help."* Even though they were half covered by burns, he could make out the next few words. *"I didn't mean to murder Giorgio, but he saw me…"* And on another piece, *"God might forgive me, but I can't."*

"It was her, after all. I can hardly believe it!" Bianca cried.

"We can rarely believe what the people we know are capable of. Whoever the killer had been, it would have surprised us." But it was obvious Bruno was shocked too.

"In the end, Marinella proved to be right," Bianca said. "Filippa killed Ivo before he could finalise their divorce. She was desperate to inherit his money… but I would never have thought her capable of murder."

"Even if her financial situation had changed dramatically and her job was less secure," Giò said, uncertain of what to believe, "I'm sure she would have had rights to a large alimony cheque."

Bruno's brows raised. "Ivo Valli Della Volpe had an army of the best lawyers, and if he'd decided to divorce, I'm sure he could have found a way to give her the bare minimum, if anything at all. He'd already got away with a couple of cases of fraud."

"I can't feel sorry for her," Bianca said, looking as pale as if all the blood had been drained from her face. Then her voice hardened. "She killed two people. Maybe her former husband was an unworthy man, but nobody deserves to die like that. And she also killed an innocent, a friend whose only fault was to have unwittingly witnessed her deeds."

"But why didn't Mr De Giorgis call out for the rest of us when he saw Filippa murdering Ivo?" Giò wondered.

"I don't think he had the time," Bruno replied. "When Filippa left the cookery class to supposedly fetch her glasses, she in reality went to the library and killed Della Volpe. De Giorgis, coming back from the watchtower, surprised her. She panicked, or pretended to, and fled back to the cliffs, and De Giorgis followed her."

"Didn't he know by then how dangerous she was?"

"You forget the affection with which he greeted her when he arrived. They were good friends. De Giorgis probably thought she had killed her former husband on an impulse, that Ivo might have provoked her. Maybe she looked so frightened that De Giorgis feared she would launch herself from the cliffs."

"And that's exactly what happened to him," Giò said, shaking her head as if to deny the horror. "The woman was a monster. She not only killed two men, but she also stopped at the pier to free a kayak, hoping we'd think De Giorgis had killed Della Volpe and run away."

"But why did she take our phones?" Bianca asked.

"She was buying time," Giò murmured, "to see if her plan had worked. But when we discovered that De Giorgis had been killed rather than come to grief trying to escape, she started to crack under the pressure. Her plan had gone wrong and the police were going to be investigating."

"About the police, shall we call them?" Bianca asked.

"Yes. Let's leave this horrific room and see if we can signal an alert using the boat's flares," Bruno said, leaving the window slightly open and closing what was left of the broken door.

THEY TOLD THE SHOCKING NEWS TO MARINELLA AND CARMELA. Marinella cried herself dry, while gulping, "That awful woman! I knew she hated us. She would have killed me too had I not secured my room properly. She was out to kill me last night."

"How can you know that?"

"I heard footsteps in the corridor."

Bruno gave her an unbelieving look, but Giò kept questioning the girl. "What time was this?"

"Around midnight, I think."

"I told you, Bruno, I heard her too, leaving her room and coming back later. Did she try to open your door, Marinella?"

"Well, not really, but I heard the footsteps outside. I think she was confused about which room was mine…"

"Now I see," Bruno said, tapping his head as if he had discovered the key to the puzzle. "She wasn't looking for your room at all, Marinella; I think she must have gone to De Giorgis's room to fetch the gun. We didn't suspect that De Giorgis had a weapon, otherwise we would have searched and locked his room."

"How can you know she found the gun in his room?" Giò asked.

"Did you not notice what type of gun it was?"

Giò shrugged. "I couldn't tell a real gun from a water pistol." But to her great irritation, Bruno kept asking questions.

"Haven't you wondered how it was possible that you could hear footsteps in the corridor outside your room, but not a gunshot in the room next door?"

They all looked at him in amazement. None of them had thought about how loud a gunshot could be.

"Well, no, I didn't think of that," Giò admitted. "I imagine a gunshot is pretty noisy, so maybe she smothered it using a pillow. I've seen it done in the movies."

Bruno shook his head. "I don't think it was high on Filippa's list of priorities not to wake us up with a gunshot."

"But I'm sure I didn't hear anything. I didn't sleep that deeply. Maybe by chance she shot herself while a clap of thunder was roaring and I didn't distinguish one from the other."

"That's a plausible explanation, but I've got another one," Bruno said with the self-assuredness of one who's on familiar ground. "The gun she used is called a PSS silent pistol, which uses special sealed cartridges that trap all the gases that, when released into the atmosphere, generate the gunshot noise. PSS guns are not that common in the Western world, but they are used in all former Soviet Union countries. They are useful to Special Forces for the elimination of specific targets without leaving clues. Not only is there virtually no noise – those guns are much more silent than any with a sound suppressor – but there are also no powder residues to contaminate the hitman's hands and clothes. An ideal weapon indeed. Officially, they are used by anti-terrorist teams, but I'm afraid they are also used for carrying out public executions."

"If Wikipedia has finished educating us all—" Giò's patience was reaching its not-very-wide limits "—could you explain to us how Filippa would have known De Giorgis had such a weapon?"

"I suspect at some point, De Giorgis must have told her he'd got a gun, and those footsteps you heard last night were Filippa going to fetch it. I don't think, Marinella, she was coming after you at all; she was looking for the gun in De Giorgis's room."

Marinella protested, "You never believe what I say! I told you all from the start that Filippa had killed Ivo, but you wouldn't listen. She may have had it in mind to carry on murdering all of us, but you'd never have listened to me. We're lucky that she decided the only other person she would kill was herself, or that gun could have killed us all."

Bianca patted Marinella on the shoulders when once more she burst into tears.

"A Russian weapon?" Giò wondered.

Bruno nodded. "De Giorgis was in Tajikistan for a long while, carrying out important journalistic investigations, so he possibly needed a weapon to defend himself. And these guns are prevalent there."

"I'd never have thought Giorgio would carry a gun with him," Bianca said.

"If you're working in certain countries, you want to take all the necessary precautions."

"This island of mine is not in Tajikistan! Frankly, I couldn't imagine Giorgio using a gun at all, and I certainly can't see the purpose of bringing one down here. But it would seem on this occasion, I have no understanding of human nature whatsoever."

"The important thing is that we're safe now," Alessandra said with a huge sigh of relief in her voice. She had done her best not to show all the tension and fear going through her mind, but like most strong people, once the danger was finally over, she could put aside her armour and show her real feelings. Her green eyes still looked tired, but they were now animated by hope.

Green eyes? Giò thought. *Who else was surprised by her green eyes, that they weren't brown?*

Bruno said, "I think it's time to go to the Saracen Tower to call for help."

"Yes, the sea is still rough, but it's definitely calming down," Caterina confirmed. "I'm going to get the flares from the boat, and we have a few in the storeroom downstairs."

"I'm coming with you," Alessandra said.

"Me too, I badly need some fresh air," said Giò. "And, Bianca, I'd love one of those headache pills of yours. Can you guys wait for me for a couple of minutes?"

As soon as they arrived in her bedroom, Bianca looked at Giò, puzzled. Asking for headache pills was out of character for Giò.

As soon as they were alone, Giò forgot all about the pills. "Bianca, how much did you know of the original story for the murder mystery weekend?"

"I really don't want to think about that stupid game, neither now nor in the future."

"Please, make an effort for me. On Friday, Alessandra said

she'd make changes to the story – she'd had a sudden inspiration and wouldn't give us the instructions until Saturday morning."

"That's true, although frankly, I couldn't see the point of changing things at the last moment. It's not easy, you know – there are the red herrings, the clues and the whole story to be put in place."

"But she went on with the changes…"

"Alessandra can be very stubborn, and I didn't even try to change her mind. After all, she was responsible for the whole thing."

"But how much did you know about the first story?"

"Very little. I get easily confused, and there were so many sub-stories and scandals intertwined, I remember almost nothing."

"And did she tell you what she'd changed in the second version of the story?"

"There was no time. I was busy enough with all the things I had to do: meals, cleaning, managing people. We have quite a few strong characters here, as you know, so I didn't even ask her what she'd changed. Also, it was more fun for me to discover things as they happened."

"That's disappointing," mumbled Giò, pensively. "I was hoping you'd be able to help me…"

"Well, I'm sorry, but when you're working with a business partner, you don't want to come across as a control freak… but wait a minute, yes, there was one thing that had changed. In the original story, I believe it was the guest Giorgio replaced, Mr Cantisani, who was meant to be the killer. I believe you were to be the killer in the second version, which seemed odd to me since you don't look much like a criminal, while Giorgio had the perfect kind of mysterious past. Then again, I guess the murderer should be someone above suspicion. But why are you asking me all this?"

"I'm piecing together a series of 'little nothings' – small things you'd never notice individually, but once you connect one of them to another, they start to add up, to fit well together. But I still don't have the whole picture, and time is running out fast…"

"Then I think it's time we called for help."

WHILE BRUNO AND CATERINA WENT TO FETCH THE FLARES FROM THE boat and fire a few from the pier, Alessandra and Giò took those from the storeroom and walked all the way to the Saracen Tower. From behind the tower, facing Praia a Mare harbour on the mainland, Giò fired the flares, and a couple of minutes after the third one had lit up the sky, she shouted triumphantly to Alessandra.

"There it is! They've replied to us. I think they're going to come to our rescue."

They waited a few more minutes, their eyes glued to the coastline till they spotted a boat moving towards the island.

"They will be here in 15 minutes. Just enough time to clarify things, Sasha," Giò said, staring at Alessandra. "When was it that De Giorgis recognised you and you decided you had to kill him? I suspect it was right from the start. He was an unexpected surprise that Bianca served on to you, wasn't he?"

"What are you talking about?" Alessandra replied, her eyes impenetrable and icy.

"He recognised you instantly, but he wasn't certain because of your excellent Italian and your green eyes. It's strange how men can be very smart, and then be deceived by small things such as coloured contact lenses. But after dinner, when he addressed you in Russian, he no longer had any doubt. Nor did you.

"Bruno didn't know that the whole discussion on Tajikistan, the drug dealers and corruption, was meant for you. He kept talking, unaware that De Giorgis was using him to send you a clear message. He knew who you were, and he'd denounce you as soon as the island was once again connected with the mainland after the storm. But that's where he made a bad error of judgement. By not alerting Bianca and the rest of us, he gifted you with extra time, and you're not someone to waste any opportunity. You had a full night to think it over, and my goodness, if you didn't come up with a complete plan for the perfect murder."

Alessandra turned her back on Giò. Unexpectedly, instead of marching down towards the harbour, she slowly headed to the belvedere from where De Giorgis had met his death.

"I think that the sad events on this island have fired everyone's imagination, kindling a collective hysteria. May I remind you that it was not only De Giorgis who died, but also two other people, and one of those had a very solid motive to do what she did? And she left us a complete confession."

Giò walked over to stand next to her. "That's what I'm saying: you didn't waste any time. That night, you rewrote the murder mystery from scratch, planning the real drama that was to be staged. In your original murder game Mr Cantisani, later substituted by Mr De Giorgis, was to be the villain. But you changed it all and gave me that part, because in the new storyline, De Giorgis had to die early. How convenient if nobody suspected there was anything odd about his temporary disappearance – it would give you extra time to play the rest of the comedy, or should I say tragedy?"

"Like what?" Alessandra stopped on the edge of the rocks, beneath which they could still distinguish De Giorgis's torn rain jacket.

"Late Friday night, I saw Filippa coming out of your room. She had just signed her own death sentence under your dictation. You were both chuckling. You made her believe she was to be the villain in the murder mystery game and she had hand-signed her confession. This is why, when you set up the suicide scene, the paper had to be partially burnt. If we had read it all, we would have understood it wasn't a real confession

ADRIANA LICIO

because, much like Judge Wargrave in Agatha Christie's novel, she confessed to not two, but nine murders!"

Alessandra shrugged her shoulders. "But you know perfectly well that you were supposed to be the villain."

But Giò was implacable. Her words kept flowing, clearing her mind on details she hadn't even been aware of.

"A smart move, having me as the *official* villain while pretending to Filippa that she was the one. That way no one would suspect her 'confession' had anything to do with the game. How convenient that only you and Filippa knew!"

"That's an absurd story, and I hope you're not going to put ideas into the heads of the police once they arrive. Why would I have killed her, and two other people I barely knew?"

"You didn't know either Ivo or Filippa, but you knew De Giorgis. You knew particularly that he knew about you and all your wicked deeds in Tajikistan. I'm sure once the police are here, they will find out that yes, you were involved in the drug trafficking. Who knows? Possibly you were the wife of one of those corrupt officials who used their position to squash smaller drug dealers and reinforce their empire. But something has gone wrong, and I'm sure the Italian Intelligence will come up with a nice story about Sasha's past..."

"Ms I-know-it-all, you still haven't replied to my question: why would I have killed Ivo and Filippa? They were complete strangers to me."

"You didn't want the police to focus their investigation on you. You knew from the start that you didn't only have to kill De Giorgis, but you had to give the police a murderer too, a completely solved case. It was unfortunate that Marinella mentioned Filippa and Ivo's incomplete divorce. That gave you a motive for someone on this island to want to kill someone else."

Sasha finally gave in. With her lazy, detached voice, she admitted, "I tried to blame it on De Giorgis, make it look like Della Volpe had been his victim. You'd all witnessed that there was a great deal of rivalry between the two."

Now, finally, Giò had all the details.

"So after the yoga lesson, you went out to ambush De Giorgis at the tower and pushed him over the cliff. How clever to get me to instruct him to stay there until we were all in the cookery lesson. Then you returned to the guesthouse and killed Della Volpe, taking him by surprise."

"Nobody would know that De Giorgis had died before Della Volpe. It was easy to make you believe it was the other way round. I would have stopped there, but De Giorgis's body got trapped among the rocks, while the kayak was carried back to the south of the island by the currents, and you all believed the murderer was still here. It wasn't a great problem, though; I'm used to preparing a Plan B, and I'd already asked Filippa to sign her confession. No one is ever careful enough in life." Alessandra's mask slipped and her last words were ferocious. "On that note, it seems to me you've not been careful at all coming up here."

"What do you mean?"

"The thing is, I also have a Plan C: to dispose of anyone sticking their noses in where they shouldn't." She got close to Giò and, before the latter could move, Alessandra had trapped her arm behind her back and twisted it in an extremely painful position. "Now, move towards the cliffs."

"If you throw me over, the others will know it was you," Giò cried, pushing her body backwards while the tips of her feet scrabbled on the unstable cliff edge, the displaced gravel falling down into the abyss.

"Rainy soil, we both slipped. They will find me down there too with a good many bruises, but miraculously alive. And I will say that you died in order to save me – I'll make a heroine and a saint out of you, so even Bianca won't suspect anything."

Alessandra pushed Giò even harder, the latter valiantly trying to resist and pull back.

"Hey, what on earth are you waiting for?" she cried.

"Is that your best trick to distract me?"

Bianca appeared from behind one of the shrubs lining the path down to the guesthouse. "In fact, it's not a trick at all. We heard your confession."

Alessandra gave a gasp as Caterina appeared beside Bianca.

"You'd better stop right there!" cried a voice from behind Giò and her assailant, arms encircling Alessandra to immobilise her.

"Ouch!" cried Giò, massaging her shoulder and arm. "You waited until the very last moment, I was starting to fear you weren't here at all."

"We wanted the whole confession." Bruno grinned, still holding Alessandra firmly even though she wasn't putting up any resistance.

Bianca approached Giò. "Are you OK? I'm not sure I've understood it all. But…"

Bruno relaxed his grip, confident that the murderer knew the battle was lost, and Alessandra thrust him over the ridge. As he tumbled over, he managed to grasp on to a shrub with his hands, but his legs were kicking in the emptiness.

Alessandra, free again, ran towards the house, howling, "You're all so stupid! I bet you left the gun unattended in the bedroom."

While Giò, Bianca and Caterina rescued poor Bruno, pulling him up from the precipice, they heard a loud thud. Behind them, Alessandra had crashed to the ground.

Carmela appeared from behind a shrub, a heavy iron skillet in her hand. "When Caterina told me you were coming up here to apprehend a killer without a weapon, I thought I'd better come along to make sure you didn't need any help. I really didn't appreciate her using one of my kitchen knives to kill a man, no matter how much I disliked him."

Bruno laughed as he made sure he was still in one piece. "Well done, Carmela, I guess you outsmarted us all." A siren sounded. "Ah, the Guardia Costiera have arrived in the harbour. And we've got quite a story to tell them."

EPILOGUE

LITTLE NOTHINGS

Once the long interview with the police was over, Giò called her sister, Agnese, who invited both her and Bianca to stay for the night. Bianca was grateful and enjoyed the company of Giò's family, but there were still too many unresolved doubts in her mind for her to be able to relax completely.

After dinner, when the rest of the family went to sleep, she lingered in the living room with Giò and Agnese and could finally fire off all her questions.

"Giò, I'm still curious. You mentioned seeing Giorgio knocking on Filippa's door on Friday night, and then Filippa said on Saturday morning she had a feeling Giorgio had wanted to speak to her. Do you think he wanted to share his suspicions about Alessandra with her?"

"I think so. They were good friends. He knew we were isolated – should he spoil your weekend when it was evident the police wouldn't be able to join us and launch an inquiry until today? He wanted advice from Filippa as to whether he should put you on your guard, or just wait for the storm to pass."

"Had De Giorgis managed to speak to Filippa," said Agnese

in dismay, "maybe it would at least have saved her life – she wouldn't have trusted Alessandra."

"That's true. Fate doesn't always work in favour of the good, I'm afraid."

Agnese shivered. To dispel the gloomy atmosphere, she asked, "How about having a taste of Granny's limoncello? This year it's excellent."

The others nodded in approval. Agnese soon returned with the bottle from the fridge and three iced tumblers. She put a finger of yellow liquid into each and they inhaled the invigorating aroma.

But Bianca was not yet satisfied with revelations, and after an appreciative sip, she asked, "Call me stupid, but could you explain to me who was killed first, Ivo or Giorgio? And when did Alessandra find the time to do them in?"

"I believe it was Alessandra who hid Marinella's camera. She knew the girl would get everyone hunting for it, and that bought her enough time to find De Giorgis in the Saracen Tower, ambush the man and push him off the cliffs. Knowing how guileful she is, we can easily imagine she knew exactly how to lure him to the edge. Or maybe she pretended she'd hurt herself and asked for help. After she killed him, she went to the pier to cut the boat cables and release the kayak."

"I remember when she came back, she was out of breath. Had she already killed Ivo at that point?"

"No, she had to make sure she'd killed her real victim first, then before joining us for the cookery lesson, she went on with her plan. She said she needed to change her clothes, but on the way upstairs, she entered the library and slipped the knife into Della Volpe's heart."

"So when Filippa entered the library in search of De Giorgis, Ivo was dead?"

"Yes, but as Filippa said, he looked like he was reading, so she just gave him a quick glance. She wanted to avoid her former husband at all costs."

"Again fate helped Alessandra, making Filippa look guilty as it seemed she was the last one to see Ivo alive."

"Correct. But even if Filippa hadn't entered the library, we always thought Ivo had been killed before De Giorgis and never suspected the real murderer."

"My goodness! I'm afraid I need one more dram, if you don't mind, Agnese?" asked Bianca, taking the limoncello bottle. "It's creamy and delicious. A secret recipe, I guess."

Agnese laughed. "We've got plenty of secrets in this family, too."

"After killing Della Volpe, Alessandra got rid of our phones, throwing them into the sea," Giò continued. It was the first time she had been able to put the pieces together, and the limoncello was certainly helping to loosen her tongue. "It was essential we should not communicate with the mainland, just in case the police looked into the pasts of each of the guests. She had to complete the *mise en scène* before we talked to the police."

"You mean staging Filippa's suicide?"

"Exactly."

"I still can't understand – how did Alessandra manage to get into Filippa's room? The door hadn't been forced, so did Filippa open it up to her? After all, Bruno had stressed that we should keep our doors locked and not open them to anyone until the morning."

"After dinner, Filippa complained of feeling drowsy. Excessively so for someone whose life could have been in danger, as all our lives were that night. I believe Alessandra had managed to drug her, likely with the pills we found in Filippa's bedroom. At dinner, she was sitting next to Filippa, so possibly she swapped their wine glasses. Drugged as she was, it was no surprise Filippa didn't answer when I tapped on her wall. Nor did she hear Alessandra coming into her room."

"But how did Alessandra manage to enter the room? That's what I don't understand."

"She had the duplicate key."

"There were only two keys for each room," Bianca insisted, "and I saw Alessandra handing Filippa the one with the yellow ring – the right colour code for Filippa's room."

"That was another of the 'little nothings' adding up. Who distributed our duplicate keys? Alessandra. She simply switched the coloured keyrings when she went to fetch them and gave Filippa the duplicate key for her own bedroom, keeping Filippa's for herself."

"My goodness, how did you realise that?"

"When we went back to our rooms, Filippa couldn't open her door as she must have been trying to use the duplicate key for Alessandra's room. Who went to help her and managed to open the door? Alessandra. I thought then it was because Filippa was too sleepy…"

"Good heavens, she tricked us right under our noses. But didn't you say you heard Filippa going to Giorgio's room later on that night?"

"In fact, it was Alessandra who went out. Hers were the footsteps I heard. It was difficult from my room to distinguish who had gone out: Filippa or Alessandra."

"So she knew Giorgio had a gun."

"No, it's as you said: De Giorgis was not the type of man who would even own a weapon, never mind bring it to your guesthouse. The gun was Alessandra's, but she was sly enough to realise it would look better if we told the police we heard Filippa go to fetch De Giorgis's weapon. You see, the whole point for Alessandra was to present a straightforward open-and-shut case; she couldn't risk the police investigating her. She was used to acting and thinking fast: she had been a spy, a terrorist, a drug trafficker, and… an actress. All skills that turned out to be very useful this weekend. And she almost managed it."

"When did you start suspecting her?"

"Only when I went to call for her this morning. For the first time, I saw her real eye colour – she hadn't had a chance to put in her contact lenses yet. And that reminded me of what De Giorgis had said during our first dinner about her eyes not being brown. Also, I couldn't understand why Filippa would write a confession, then burn it. And if she had, why would she be careless enough to leave entire parts readable? Then there was the Russian gun. Three people might have such a weapon: Bruno, De Giorgis, Alessandra."

"Now that you've made me think, what about the flower vase? Was that evidence?"

"Did you notice that too?"

"Not at the time, but now you've made me rethink all that happened…"

"Exactly. When Alessandra saw De Giorgis, she was shocked and the flowerpot slipped from her hands. Della Volpe thought he had turned around too suddenly and had caused her to drop it, when in fact, he hadn't even touched her. As soon as he asked her, 'Was it me?' she used that to cover up her reaction."

"How awful," Agnese commented. "She had an answer for everything."

"She even pretended she was in favour of spending the night together when the lights went off," said Bianca.

"Whenever I felt that things weren't quite as they seemed, she was the common denominator." Giò felt it was her place to close the conversation, before the limoncello bottle was completely empty. "True, it was always something small and apparently meaningless, but those 'little nothings' eventually led me to the real story."

THE CAPTAIN'S VOICE BROKE INTO HER THOUGHTS ON HER FLIGHT back to London. "You can now unfasten your seatbelts."

"The take-off went well," said the bulky young man sitting

beside her. He seemed determined to speak to Giò, despite the fact her earphones were sending out a clear 'Do not disturb' message. She pretended not to hear him, but undeterred, he tapped her on the shoulder.

She unplugged one ear bud and looked at him with her coldest stare.

"The take-off went well," he repeated innocently, eager to share his thoughts with someone.

"Clearly. If it hadn't, you wouldn't be tapping on my shoulder," Giò replied icily, plugging her earphones in again. Not only did departures bring out the worst in her, but Fate always seemed to make sure she'd be sitting next to a jerk, which didn't ease things a tiny bit. She thought savagely of Paul Theroux, who always seemed to end up having enlightening conversations with his fellow travellers.

Tap tap. She opened her eyes.

"Have you ever been to London? This is my first time. I'm hoping to work there as a pizza chef. My mother's third cousin has invited me to share his flat. Apparently they can't find decent pizza chefs there. Imagine that – a city of nine million people and not one who can make a decent pizza."

She closed her eyes and turned her back on him, but five minutes later, he tapped on her shoulder again. Giò turned in a fury, determined to put an end to the jerk's requests, but he whispered softly, "I think you want to rest a little. I'm going to the back to chat with some of our fellow travellers. Is it OK if I leave you alone for a while?"

Giò nodded, so full of gratitude that for the first time, the shadow of a smile appeared on her face. Saying goodbye to Agnese, her nephew and niece, and of course Granny had been harder than usual. She knew that if Dorian had his way, she wouldn't return to Maratea for a long time. When she was in London, she didn't realise how much she missed home, but whenever she went back…

Departures had become bitter pills to swallow!

And it wasn't only her family she missed, but the relaxed way people talked to each other in the shops, the cafés, even on the streets. It was the Mediterranean Sea, the combination of the high rocky mountains and the gulf, the helm forest, the broom in flower. The perfume of fig trees mixed with carobs and jasmine; the yellow lemons hanging from branches for most of the year; the women who could dispute the traditional way to prepare a ragù sauce for hours.

She would even miss Agnese's customers, watching them – always from a safe distance – walking in and out of her perfumery with their laughter and their tears, their problems and their joys. And their quirkiness too, like Cristina Agata who, only a week before Giò's fateful trip, had told Agnese that the idea of a murder weekend based on *And Then There Were None* on the Isola di Pino was not a good idea, unless the guests were actively looking for trouble. Giò smiled, still incredulous at the accuracy of local gossips.

She understood why it had been so important for Bianca to go back home after years in Turin. There comes a time when you really miss home. With the murders on the island hitting the headlines, Bianca had feared that she would be forced to sell the guesthouse and imagine a different future for herself, but the reservations had started to flood in. Bianca had warned her guests that no murder mystery weekends would ever happen on the island again, but it seemed the national news had worked as the best promotional campaign conceivable. Caterina and Carmela had confirmed that they were willing to stay, and they had definitely proved themselves to be two worthy people to have around. And Storm and Thunder would undoubtedly enjoy having more quirky humans around to observe.

But hey, at least her family would all be coming to London for her wedding in October. After ten years together, she and Dorian were finally going to get married, move into their new home and live happily ever after.

THE END

READ MORE... AND GET YOUR COPY OF MURDER ON THE ROAD.

MURDER ON THE ROAD

AN ITALIAN VILLAGE MYSTERY - BOOK 1

1

A PAINFUL TRAIN JOURNEY

Giò pretended to be engrossed in her book, but it did not help.

"Oh, you should see the dress we chose for her!" the fat blonde lady sitting in front of her continued mercilessly, her voice shrill. "She looks like a Hollywood actress. I can't imagine Duccio's face when he sees her. He wanted to come along, but tradition forbids the future husband seeing the bride's dress before the wedding."

Giò nodded, trying not to seem encouraging. She'd had enough of the woman's talk, which had started as the train left Naples, and was still as lively one and a half hours later. There were another 30 long minutes to go before they reached Sapri, and there was a real risk they would end up sitting next to each other on the regional train to Maratea, Giò's hometown.

Giò did not return the woman's smile and once again pretended to be absorbed in her reading. But her travelling companion, who had introduced herself as Mrs Di Bello, didn't seem to notice and carried on as if Giò had shown great interest.

"Duccio let Dora choose the wedding venue, the menu, the decorations. He totally trusts her refined taste." Mrs Di Bello elongated her vowels, sounding like a soprano singer practising the higher notes on the scale. "He's sooo in love with heeer that he said they would go whereeever she wanted tooo for their honeymoon. He said that whereeever she chose would be nothing short of peeerfect."

For a fraction of a second, Giò visualised how difficult things had been with Dorian. Whatever she suggested "could always be improved upon", by which he meant she should put aside her own desires to leave plenty of room for his ideas and plans. But she sent the thought away. Not now. Not when she was finally going home. All she wanted was a little quiet time to let it sink in...

No, stop those thoughts! They were too painful right now. She longed to gaze at the familiar landscape, knowing that after 15 years of living abroad, she was finally coming back home, maybe for good. But she dared not raise her eyes from the book.

"And the house – he bought her the house of her dreams. It has a stunning view of the gulf. It's such a big house, too. If I think how Mr Di Bello and I started when we got married. We only had two small rooms and we weren't sure we could pay the next month's rent. But these two young ones, life has been generous to them. Duccio comes from a long line of lawyers, and he's continuing the family tradition. It is not only the money, though; he is sooo much in love with Dora. In the three years of their engagement, they've only had one major fight.

"I mean, it was about something so stupid, I can't even remember what. But Dora was so angry, she left him. And when he came to ours, tears in his eyes, begging her to reconsider, to go back to him, she said she would have to think about it. He kept sending flowers and letters and ringing her. In the end, they made up. And they've never argued since."

Giò thought she wouldn't mind asking Dora for a little womanly advice. She clearly knew about winning a man's heart. But Giò was careful not to show any sign of interest; she longed for silence and hoped there would come a point when Mrs Di Bello would run out of things to say.

Unfortunately, the woman needed no encouragement to carry on. "A week ago, they passed a jewellery shop and Dora saw a beautiful bracelet. The price was outrageous, and she did not think for a moment... she simply found it beautiful. The next morning, Duccio gave me a little box and asked me to let Dora find it with her breakfast. Oh, I've never seen a man more in love..."

The gods were determined to punish Giò further. Not only did she have a broken heart, not only had she called off her forthcoming wedding after an engagement of 10 years, not only was she leaving behind all she had built, but she was supposed to listen to this nauseating love story. Mrs Di Bello was one of those people who merely needed the sight of two ears to tell all she had to tell. She noticed none of the younger woman's hurt and carried on pitilessly.

"I can't wait for them to have kids."

"Do they plan to have any? Is Duccio happy with that?" For the first time, Giò was asking questions.

"Sure they do. Dora wants to have a couple of children if God will bless her."

"And Duccio?" Giò put her book down, stubbornly determined to find a fault with the perfect couple.

"Oh, he is such a considerate man. He said pregnancy is so demanding on a woman that he will never put Dora under pressure. When she feels she's ready..."

"Maybe he is so understanding because he does not want any kids." *At least I can instil some doubt in her mind,* Giò thought maliciously, but Mrs Di Bello's faith was unshaken.

"Oh no, he says he'd love to be a father, but that he will let Dora choose when."

This was too much. Duccio had to be a man with no backbone, just living for his wife. He was rich; he was considerate; he was the kind of man who did not exist.

"I will show you a picture of the two, as it must seem like you know them by now." Before Giò could say anything, Mrs Di

Bello had pulled out her mobile to show her the ideal couple. He looked like Prince Charming (Giò had hoped he would be repulsive) and she was pretty. Not a stunning beauty, but she had an expressive, determined little face, and she certainly knew how to use make-up.

"He's so much in love with her."

Giò raised her chin in the air. Had Agnese, her sister, been there, she would have recognised that the gesture meant trouble. Giò's lips stretched into a grin, her jaw jutting forward as if to direct the incoming storm, and most telling of all, a flash passed through her eyes, turning them from deep green to a feline yellow.

She spoke in a cold voice. "Do you think so? I hope not. Because, as the entire world knows, when a man acts like that, when he shows nothing but blind devotion, he is only doing it to reassure the bride, her family and close friends that they are living the perfect dream." Her voice rose steadily. "Beware! It's only a smokescreen to hide all kinds of treacherous things. Do you believe he hasn't got a lover? That he is not painting this cutest of family pictures so he can enjoy his misdemeanours in peace? You cannot be that naïve. If I were you, I would advise my daughter to keep her eyes wide open, to get out of this fairy tale mood, and check his mobile whenever she gets a chance. If she finds nothing incriminating, he's probably got another phone."

Mrs Di Bello stared at her as if Giò was possessed. She tried to get a few words in edgeways, but the younger woman was on a roll. Giò's voice rose so much that all the passengers in the carriage started to listen in. Two women, though clearly surprised at Giò's audacity, were nodding in approval.

"By the way, did I say *a* lover? If I did, I didn't mean there would only be one. For the scoundrel to behave so meekly, to give your daughter all that you mentioned, surely he has more than one. Tell your daughter not to waste her time on shop windows, but to check where the rest of the money goes. What does he do when he is absent? For how long is he away? Is it really for work? Because, you see," and at this point, Giò stretched out her arm, palm raised to silence her horrified companion, "every time a man comes in with a present, you can be sure he's done something bad. Every flower, every box of chocolates is a bad sign, but jewellery is the worst sign of all. Every sugary message is to sweeten up your daughter when he's just left the arms of another woman!"

Mrs Di Bello had been trying to interrupt, but now she was silent, afraid that the lunatic opposite her might harm her. She had been confiding in this madwoman, telling her all about her lovely daughter for almost two hours. Grabbing her bags, Mrs Di Bello tried to get up and go, but Giò had not finished yet. She stood up and barred the older woman's way.

"And, you didn't ask a single thing of me. You spoke for two hours about your silly daughter and her happiest of weddings. Did you stop for a second to think whether the woman in front of you had also been about to get married? Yes, in a month's time. And did you stop to think that maybe something had gone terribly wrong?" Here, Giò had to pause and draw breath, her eyes watery. But her anger was such that she held back the tears that had never come when she'd wanted them.

"Have you wondered if maybe this silent lady," and she gestured towards the pale woman sitting across the aisle, close to the opposite window, "has suffered at the hands of a bastard pretending to be the best man ever?"

The pale woman nodded vigorously in approval, and so did a few other women in the carriage.

"That's so terribly selfish of you, to think only of your own – fake – happiness and forget the misery of thousands of women around you."

The whole compartment burst into loud applause. Giò had not realised there were so many women who'd had to endure Mrs Di Bello's tales too. Somebody from behind her shouted, "Well said, sister."

Finally, all her energy left her, and she dropped back in her seat, trembling with both rage and pain. Mrs Di Bello was free to run away with her heavy luggage, searching for a safe place in another carriage. Maybe this time, she would be more careful about what she said. That is, if she said anything at all.

Giò did not have much time to think. Once the train had passed through the last tunnel, the view opened up to reveal the coastline that was so familiar to her. 10 minutes later, it arrived at Sapri station and her heartbeat quickened. The regional train was waiting on the opposite platform.

She took the first available seat next to a window, knowing full well that Mrs Di Bello would be careful to avoid entering the same carriage. The train started and her eyes gazed at the most dramatic coastline she had ever seen, despite her many wanderings. High, rocky mountains in unique pinkish colours loomed like walls, plunging down into the sea beneath. A few pine forests and scattered clumps of vegetation faced the Policastro Gulf, watched over by the majestic profile of Mount Bulgheria. The Statue of Christ the Redeemer, the symbol and protector of her seaside town, Maratea, was not yet in sight, but a few more tunnels and she would be home.

"AUNTIEEE!" A LITTLE RED-HAIRED GIRL WITH TWO PIGTAILS RAN AT full speed along the platform and dived into Giò's arms. They squeezed each other tightly.

"I thought you wouldn't recognise me," Giò said, laughing.

"I did, and I spotted you long before all the others." Lilia proudly indicated the rest of the family, who were coming along the platform behind her.

"They're all here? My goodness."

"When Mum said she was coming, we all said we'd come too. Uncle Valerio could not make it, though, he is very busy," Lilia explained.

Luca, Lilia's brother, reached them. He was 12 by now and wanted to uphold a certain image, but when his auntie twinkled at him, he just had to hug her. It wasn't bad to be a kid every now and then.

"Granny!" Giò shouted.

"My little child!" Only Granny could call her that. In her arms, Giò recognised the familiar perfume of violets and face powder that had comforted her since childhood. Granny had pure white wavy hair, with a few rebel bangs hanging around her heart-shaped face, a nicely pointed chin and lively grey eyes, and she was as thin as her granddaughter.

"Such a stupid man. How could he hurt my little flower?" Granny added, caressing Giò's face.

"Granny, you promised!" Agnese chastised her. "Not here, not now."

Granny sighed; Giò tried to smile.

"And I'd say she's more of a cactus than a flower, anyway."

Giò pretended to be shocked, and Lilia laughed.

"You're just as skinny as ever. Not even the UK could give you a few curves." Agnese continued looking at her sister's slender figure and compared it with her own plumpness, but the arms that closed around Giò spoke of softness, understanding, happiness finally to be able to comfort her in person rather than over a Skype call.

"Can I welcome my sister-in-law?" asked Nando. Pulling all the others away, he hugged Giò in his massive arms. "I've only got this moment, you see," he added, looking at the rest of the family. "Give them five minutes, and she and her sister will be teasing me as usual."

They all laughed.

"Granny has made some delicious spaghetti alle vongole. For the second course, we're having stuffed squid," Lilia giggled.

"And I'm sure there will be dessert from Panza," Luca added. Family meals were a serious thing here in Southern Italy.

"Is this all the luggage you have?" asked Nando, lifting Giò's bag. It was large, but still only a single bag.

"A courier will deliver six boxes of stuff during the week. All the rest I left in a storage unit. I've rented the space for three months with the possibility of renewal. I'll see to that."

"What a waste of money. This time you're here to stay!" Granny said.

Agnese stared at her with such intensity that the 80-year-old lady fell silent, which was unusual for her.

"Was your journey OK?" Agnese changed the subject.

"I'd rather answer another question." Giò laughed guiltily, feeling suddenly ashamed of what she had done.

"Why, Auntie?" asked Lilia.

"Let's say I had a very chatty companion, and maybe I overdid it in order to keep her quiet!" Giò raised her brows comically until they almost reached her hairline. Everyone laughed, both at her funny face and because they knew all about her temper.

DINNER WAS A FAMILY OCCASION, AND WAS GREAT FUN, WITH Agnese and Granny competing to refill Giò's dishes as she finished each course. They were all laughing and joking, recalling childhood memories, and Giò realised how stupid she had been. Dorian had not liked her family, nor Maratea.

"It's a good place for a day trip, but my goodness, I'd go out of my mind if I were to hang around here for longer than 24 hours," he used to say. So she had not gone home for the last few Christmases, as she used to. She knew her family had felt a mixture of disappointment and relief whenever she'd announced she would visit them, but no, Dorian could not make it.

Her family had never liked Dorian, she was positive about that, but they had always welcomed him so as not to hurt her. Well, except for Granny. Every now and then, a few harsh words would come out of her mouth, and Agnese would try to justify them.

"She's just protective; she's afraid he might not make you happy."

Or had Agnese been speaking her own mind too? None of this mattered any longer. In the future, no man would ever keep Giò away from her family, no matter what.

"I want to visit Sapri tomorrow morning. Should I use the train since the road is closed?" Giò asked while helping her sister to tidy up the kitchen.

"You said you wanted to stop at Mum and Dad's, so you'd be better off driving. Once you've finished there, park where they closed the road, just above the cemetery. You catch the bus to Sapri on the other side. I've left a timetable on your desk."

"Can I walk across the closed road?"

"Technically you can't, but everyone does, especially the folks in Acquafredda. There are too few trains. If you want company, we could go together on Sunday."

"No, I need some time alone. I also need a new SIM card. I'll be fine."

Giò went up to the attic above her sister's house. The same main doorway on the street led to three independent apartments: Granny lived on the ground floor, Agnese on the first floor. The second floor was a two-room attic with a sunny terrace. Agnese used to rent it to tourists, but it was to be Giò's space till she decided what to do next.

"You should live here forever," Lilia had said.

From her terrace, Giò could see a few lights from the fishermen's boats out at sea. Putting on a shawl, because on a September night the temperature could drop in Maratea, she went out to smell the fresh air. The silence was absolute. The air was sweet. She was home.

2

ROCKFALLS AND LIPSTICKS

The next morning, the slim figure of Elena Errico hurried across the cobblestones, despite her high heels. Her boss's wife, Mrs Rivello, had called her the night before; Mrs Rivello didn't feel well, but she needed to hand in some documents to the school office. The closed road was a pain; it meant Elena leaving Mrs Rivello's car in Acquafredda and taking the bus to Sapri. Better get it over with as soon as possible.

She got in the car and drove along the state road, passing through Cersuta. Here the coastline was particularly wild and the houses were few, mostly hidden by the vegetation. The rock walls plunged into the sea from a vertiginous height, making it an area of outstanding natural beauty in any weather. Maybe soon, she would be able to buy a house here. Her own house. Yes, later she would meet him, and she would talk to him. Well, it would be more of a reminder than a talk.

She reached Acquafredda, went through the rocky tunnel and stopped the car in front of the closed road. On the left-hand side there was a parking space containing three cars. The area on the right had to be left free for work vehicles and staff. But Mrs Rivello, who went to Sapri almost every morning, had her own parking space on that side. After all, it was a partner firm of Mr

Rivello's company that had been awarded the road securing works.

Today there were no workers, though. Following the geotechnical site assessment, the firm was waiting for the last of the bureaucratic procedures to be completed. Then work would start on rock scaling: removing loose rocks from the slope, laying new catch fences to intercept rockfalls, cleaning the road, and finally repairing it.

A small niche on the right, half hidden by the vegetation, was free for Mrs Rivello's car. Elena parked, switched off the engine and searched for her bag on the passenger seat to check she had everything. She had not even removed her seatbelt when a movement from the mountain above startled her. By instinct, her hand grasped the door handle, but the seatbelt held her captive. She could not escape.

Elena did not have time to think: she just felt adrenaline bursting through her body. Could it even be called pain? A huge rock had fallen on the top of Mrs Rivello's car and crushed the life out of her.

Read More... and get your copy of *Murder On The Road.*

Is there any way a reader may help a newbie author? Yes! **Please leave a review of** *"And Then There Were Bones"* **on your favourite eStore, Bookbub or Goodreads.** It doesn't matter how long or short; even a single sentence could say it all. We might be in a digital era, but **this old world of ours still revolves around word of mouth.** A review allows a book to leave the shadow of the unknown and introduces it to other passionate readers.

Grazie :)

JOIN THE MARATEA MURDER CLUB

You'll get exclusive content:

- **Giò Brando's Maratea Album** – photos of her favourite places and behind-the-scenes secrets
- **A Maratea Map** – including most places featured in the series
- **Adriana Licio's News** – new releases, news from Maratea, but no spam – Giò would loathe it!
- **Cosy Mystery Passion:** a place to share favourite books, characters, tips and tropes

Sign up to:
www.adrianalicio.com/murderclub

BOOK 1: MURDER ON THE ROAD

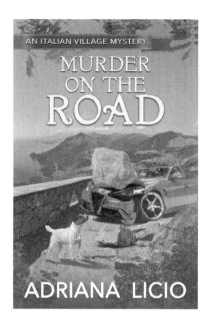

—

Can murder be the cure for a broken heart?

Returning to her quaint hometown in Italy following the collapse of her engagement, feisty travel writer Giò Brando just wants some peace and quiet. Instead, she finds herself a suspect in a brutal murder.

Anxious to clear her name, Giò embarks on her own investigation, eavesdropping on the gossip in her sister's perfumery and the cafés of Maratea as she pieces together the evidence. But something about the case isn't adding up. Or is Giò allowing her attraction to a fellow suspect to distract her?

Wanting to distance herself from danger, Giò keeps her feelings in check. But when new evidence turns the whole case on its head, danger is exactly what is waiting for her.

~

Murder on the Road is the first book in the compelling and heartwarming *An Italian Village Mystery* series. If you want a taste of Mediterranean village life, take a bite of this tasty treat, and bury your nose in the mysterious world of essences and perfumes.

MORE BOOKS FROM ADRIANA LICIO

THE HOMESWAPPERS SERIES

0 - Castelmezzano, The Witch Is Dead – Prequel to the series

1 - The Watchman of Rothenburg Dies: A German Travel Mystery

2 - A Wedding and A Funeral in Mecklenburg : A German Cozy Mystery

3 - An Aero Island Christmas Mystery: A Danish Cozy Mystery

4 – Prague, A Secret From The Past – coming in Spring 2021

AN ITALIAN VILLAGE MYSTERY SERIES

0 - And Then There Were Bones. The prequel to the *An Italian Village Mystery* series.

1 - Murder on the Road Returning to her quaint hometown in Italy following the collapse of her engagement, feisty travel writer Giò Brando just wants some peace and quiet. Instead, she finds herself a suspect in a brutal murder.

2 A Fair Time for Death is a mystery set during the Autumn Chestnut Fair in Trecchina, a mountain village near Maratea, involving a perfume with a split personality, a disappearing corpse, a disturbing secret from the past and a mischievous goat.

3 - A Mystery Before Christmas A haunting Christmas song from a faraway land. A child with striking green eyes. A man with no past. A heartwarming mystery for those who want to breathe in the delicious scents and flavours of a Mediterranean December.

4 - Peril at the Pellicano Hotel – A group of wordsmiths, a remote hotel. Outside, the winds howl and the seas rage. But the real danger lurks within.

More books to come in Summer 2021

ALSO

"When The Clock Chimes Two" a short story in *"Mystery Follows Her"* a collection of intriguing and light-hearted stories by nine award-winning and best-selling authors from across the globe. My own story features Giò Brando, Agnese and a mischievous perfume with a mesmerising name "Passage d'Enfer". It can be a good introduction to the *An Italian Village Mystery* series.

"Life Lines" a three-page story featuring Giò Brando and her Grandmother in **"Stop the World: Snapshot From a Pandemic"** 40 authors from around the world set out to record their innermost feelings -- to offer inspiring, heartfelt, creative takes on the Covid-19 pandemic. Crime fiction, elegant and angry poetry, and gut-wrenching personal essays: all paint a picture of the year and help us make sense of the sacrifices we've made in 2020.

GLOSSARY

BRUSCHETTA – plural bruschette: a slice of toasted bread (possibly cooked on the barbecue or grilled or roasted in a pizza oven), seasoned with garlic, olive oil, sliced fresh tomatoes, anchovies, olives, etc…

CAVATELLI: are a common pasta prepared in the southern part of Italy. Their name comes from 'cavo', meaning 'hollow' in Italian, so quite literally they are 'little hollows'. The hollow space is created by the quick hands of the chef rolling a small dough stick on a pasta board.

    The size of cavatelli may vary according to the technique the cook uses – one, two or three fingers – and the dish they're preparing. A fierce debate rumbles on endlessly as to whether one should use one or two finger cavatelli with bean soup.

CORNETTO – plural cornetti: This is the equivalent of a French croissant. I have to admit it was the French who invented them, but they're very popular in Italy too.

ISOLA DI PINO: Isola is the equivalent of island, so the Isola di Pino is Pino's Island. Pino can be a person's first name (often short for Giuseppe: Giuseppino - small Giuseppe - Pino), but it's also the Italian name for Pine Tree.

LIMONCELLO: It's a very popular liqueur in Southern Italy, typical of all the places where lemons are cultivated. It's often homemade, and each household will have his own recipe. The important thing is to have lemons that have not been treated since the skin is also used to give the liqueur its sparkling aroma.

RAGU: you won't find Bolognese sauce in Southern Italy restaurants (if you do, it's a sure sign the restaurant is meant for tourists). Our version of Bolognese sauce is called ragù and it's not made of mincemeat, but with different pieces of meat or the so-called involtini/braciole (meat cuts wrapped around a filling – our family recipes call for ham, parsley, parmigiano, raisins and pine nuts).

SARACEN TOWER – This is what we call watchtowers on the coast, and we've got plenty of them. Imagine that on the Maratea coast alone, which is no more than 30 kilometres long, I've counted over 10 of them. But don't be misled by the name. They were not built by the Saracens, but by the local people wanting to defend themselves from pirate attacks. In fact, 'watchtowers' would be a more appropriate name, but to us they are le Torri Saracene – the Saracen Towers.

TORTE as in Le Torte di Bea means Beatrice's pies or cakes.

If you have found other Italian words in the story and would like to know what they mean, please let me know.

Contact me on:
    Twitter: @adrianalici
    Mail: me@adrianalicio.com

ABOUT THE AUTHOR

Adriana Licio lives in the Apennine Mountains in southern Italy, not far from Maratea, the seaside setting for her first cosy series, *An Italian Village Mystery.*

She loves loads of things: travelling, reading, walking, good food, small villages, and home swapping. A long time ago, she spent six years falling in love with Scotland, and she has never recovered. She now runs her family perfumery, and between a dark patchouli and a musky rose, she devours cosy mysteries.

She resisted writing as long as she could, fearing she might get carried away by her fertile imagination – she was already renowned for living in the clouds. But one day, she found an alluring blank page and the words flowed in the weird English she'd learned in Glasgow.

Adriana finds peace for her restless, enthusiastic soul by walking in nature with her adventurous golden retriever Frodo and her hubby Giovanni.

Do you want to know more?
You can also stay in touch on:
www.adrianalicio.com

facebook.com/adrianalicio.mystery

twitter.com/adrianalici

amazon.com/author/adrianalicio

bookbub.com/authors/adriana-licio

A Q&A WITH ADRIANA LICIO

How do you pronounce Giò?

The same way you'd pronounce Jo.

Why did you call your main character Giò?

My instinctive reply would be because it works well with the surname Brando, a surname that captured my imagination a few years ago while I was sipping a cappuccino at Iannini's bar in Maratea. But I have to acknowledge that my life has always been full of Giovannis. It was my grandfather's name (and my great-great-grandfather's), and it's now the name of my brother and the man I've shared my life with for the past 20 years. My dog's first son was named Giò, too.

And of course there's Jo – Josephine March, whose deeds will accompany me forever, and now Joanna Penn, whose writing course I joined when I decided I really wanted to write a book. Without Joanna, this book would not even exist.

Does the Isola di Pino really exist?

Since I was a child, I've been fascinated by the Island of Dino in Calabria, laid out beyond the beach of Praia a Mare where I went camping with my family. It looks distant and full of mysteries, but for the purpose of my book, it happens to be just a bit too close to the mainland (100 metres or so, I believe). So I decided that I would push it further out into the sea, and to avoid confusion, change its name from Dino to Pino and have done with it.

Today, Pino and Dino are both common first names, but the island name Dino supposedly came from the ancient Greek word *dina* meaning a storm or a vortex – a discovery that fired up my imagination.

I've never been to the island, and I doubt there's a lighthouse, but there are the grottos, the ruins of an ancient tower, and yes, there was a guesthouse too. Whether such a story as I have told has ever occurred there, I'm not sure, but the island has been confiscated by the police and the residence never opened again, which is a pity. And that's why I like books more than reality.

Do you take inspiration from real people?

In order to stay creative, I don't want to involve real people at all, especially the people I know.

There are exceptions, of course. A person who kindles my imagination may be the stranger on the bus, a lady I've never spoken to, someone making a weird remark in a café. From that spark I can create a fictional character. But on the whole, unlike places, real people bog down the imagination. The more I know them, the less I have the freedom to do with them as I wish.

Why are Italian words not italicised in the story?

In the first draft of *Murder on the Road*, I did, as is normal writing style, use italics for all non-English words. But when I saw the words *carabiniere, maresciallo, brigadiere* in italics over and over again, I felt they were like a punch in the stomach. I asked Giò, and she said that since she speaks Italian and lives in Italy, she couldn't see the point of highlighting words that she would use over and over again. She also said she wanted you, the readers, to feel as close to Maratea as possible, and italicising Italian words might have the opposite effect.

Giò's argument convinced both me and, importantly, Alison Jack, my heroic editor. "So be it," we said. We also included a Glossary to help you out. But the last word is for you, the reader. Please let us know if you (don't) agree with Giò's choice.

More questions?

If you have any other questions you would like to ask me, feel free to contact me. I might even add your question to the Q&A page in my next novel. Or you might like to read the interview Giò did with me on **my website!**

Contact me on:
    Twitter: @adrianalici
    Mail: me@adrianalicio.com

Printed in Great Britain
by Amazon

84684755R00082